SECRETS IN THE GRAVE

Karen Ann Hopkins

ISBN: 1515286533
ISBN 13: 9781515286530
Library of Congress Control Number: 2015912606
Createspace Independent Publishing Platform
North Charleston, South Carolina

PRAISE FOR LAMB TO THE SLAUGHTER & WHISPERS FROM THE DEAD

"A well-crafted tale of murder begotten by the collision of two incompatible worlds." Kirkus reviews.

"*Lamb to the Slaughter* was an easy, enjoyable read that I completely enjoyed. I was over the moon excited to hear that there will be more books in this series. Serenity and Daniel will solve cases involving Amish communities throughout the Midwest!" Caffeinated Book Reviewer

"I would highly, highly recommend this one…From the mystery, the characters and the writing this is a fantastic book! I can't wait for book two!" Lose Time Reading

"From the prologue to the last chapters, Lamb to the Slaughter had me instantly hooked. Ms. Hopkins is a master at pacing and setting up her stories in a way that has readers connected to both the characters and the story line." Love-Life-Read

"This book had it all!! Murder, mystery, forbidden romance and left you needing to read the next book in the series ASAP!! Loved this book!" Curling Up With a Good Book

"Karen Ann Hopkins has delivered with Lamb to the Slaughter. I love the uniqueness she brings to the mystery genre, and I

will DEFINITELY be reading more from her in the future."
Unabridged Bookshelf

"The characters are complex and dimensional, whether they
have a large or smaller part to play in this story, and it really
added such a richness that I enjoyed." Bewitched Bookworms

"Lamb to the Slaughter is a must read for fans of mystery
novels. Karen Ann Hopkins made me a fan with her YA
Temptation series, and she's made me an even bigger fan with
this murder mystery." Actin' Up With Books

"An intriguing tale full of mystery and suspense....LAMB TO
THE SLAUGHTER had me thinking and rethinking the entire time." I Read Indie!

"I'm so glad that this is going to be a series; because it's one
of the greatest murder mysteries that I've read in a long time."
Little Miss Drama Queen

"Simply put Karen Ann Hopkins, takes her readers to a new
level of Amish fiction and suspense." Deitre Helvey Owens at
Once Upon a Twilight

"Lamb to the Slaughter will keep you at the edge of your seat.
Don't miss this nail biting experience!" Her Book Thoughts

"Lamb to the Slaughter is a stunningly suspenseful read that
will have you flipping pages long after bedtime. You won't
want to miss it!" Bittersweet Enchantment

"Whispers from the Dead is my favorite book so far this year!" Unabridged Bookshelf

"I give Whispers from the Dead a 5 out of 5! This installment explores how big city problems don't necessarily stay in the big city...it makes for a steamy and seductive read." Bewitched Bookworms

"Loved this book! This book gives you everything...kids buying illegal narcotics, revenge burnings, overdoses, secrets, lies, kidnapping and several shootings, and all in one northern touristy Amish community." Curling Up With a Good Book

"Whispers from the Dead is a success!" Her Book Thoughts

BOOKS BY KAREN ANN HOPKINS

Serenity's Plain Secrets
in reading order
LAMB TO THE SLAUGHTER
WHISPERS FROM THE DEAD
SECRETS IN THE GRAVE

Wings of War
in reading order
EMBERS
GAIA

The Temptation Novels
in reading order
TEMPTATION
BELONGING
FOREVER
RACHEL'S DEPCEPTION
SUMMER'S SONG (2016)

For Anthony.
Your generous spirit never ceases to amaze me. Thank you for everything.

ACKNOWLEDGEMENTS

As always, I'm thankful to Jenny Zemanek of Seedlings Design Studio for another wonderful cover, Amanda Shofner for her excellent editorial skills, and Heather Miller for her attention to detail. I'm proud to have all of you as part of my team!

Much love and thanks to my children: Luke, Cole, Lily, Owen, and Cora. I couldn't ask for better children...or friends. And I'm always grateful for my mom's insight and wisdom. I wouldn't have written nine books without your guidance. I love you.

Opal, your enthusiasm for my books and your personal connection to the Amish have made you the best critique partner. Much appreciation for your support and friendship. You're one in a million.

A special shout out for the readers and bloggers who have promoted my books. Deitre from A Leisure Moment, Joli from Actin' Up With Books, Beckie from Bittersweet Enchantment, and Beth from Curling Up With a Good Book are a few of the special people who have helped make my books successful through their blogs and word-of-mouth advertising. Your recommendations have been instrumental in spreading the word. Thank you!

And finally, my deepest, heartfelt gratitude to my husband, Jay, the best man in the world. Without you, I never would have made it this far.

"Success is sweeter and sweeter if long delayed and gotten through many struggles and defeats."

~Amos Bronson Alcott

PROLOGUE

July 10, 2005
Black Willow Amish Settlement, Ohio

The contraction rolled through Robyn's lower back, hips and thighs with stabbing pain. She took a deep breath and concentrated on pushing harder. This was the fifth baby she'd brought into the world. She was relieved the labor was progressing quicker than the other four had. Each subsequent birth was hastier than the last, but the suffering was much the same. Oh, how she despised this part. It felt as if the baby was wrestling, trying to crawl its way further inside, and no amount of pushing would dislodge its stubbornness. It didn't want to leave the warmth and security of its mother's womb. She could hardly blame the infant, but with the passing of each stinging contraction, she was losing patience. As the last pain subsided to an uncomfortable throbbing, she said a silent prayer that it would be over soon.

"Come now, Robyn. You're no stranger to this business. You're practically an expert." Ada Mae pressed the cool, damp cloth against Robyn's forehead. "It's nearly noon. You must push harder, dear."

Robyn scowled at her sister-in-law. The younger woman knew her herbal remedies, but she resented her demanding tone. Ada Mae had never been pregnant. She hadn't experienced the agonizing pain a woman endured bringing her child into the world. Robyn bit her lip, keeping quiet. Ada Mae had been recently widowed. Her husband had met an unfortunate end when a young Belgian horse he was shoeing kicked him in the face.

As the pinching pain of another contraction built, Robyn pitied her sister-in-law. Not only had the poor woman lost her husband, but she also had no children of her own to comfort her in the days to come. And she never would have any. Ada Mae's womb was barren.

"I want to wait for Jonas. He delivered his other children. This one should be no different," Robyn said through clenched teeth.

Ada Mae sighed, shaking her head. "There's no telling when Jonas will be back from the Troyer's farm. Little Sarah Troyer was awfully sick. I'd imagine he'll be there for a while."

Robyn remained silent, suffering through the cramping without pushing. When the pains diminished, she fell back onto the pillows with a groan. "I don't think I can do it without him. This young'un's being difficult," Robyn said weakly.

"We are going on two hours since Robyn began pushing, perhaps it's time to call the driver to take her to the hospital," Mrs. Gingerich suggested into Ada Mae's ear.

Ada Mae shrugged the gray-haired woman off. "This is Robyn's fifth child. There's no need for the cost of a hospital. My brother would have a fit we failed to do our duty here," Ada Mae chastised. She swiveled to Robyn. "A little more effort on Robyn's part and we'll be hearing the squalling of a baby soon enough."

Robyn rolled her eyes. "I could use some more of that tea. It might help with the pain."

"All right. It certainly can't hurt." Ada Mae flicked her head in Mrs. Gingerich's direction. "Pour her another cup."

Even though Mrs. Gingerich was thirty years older than Ada Mae, she did as she was told without question. With hands gnarled from age, she poured the last of the contents of the tea pot into the mug. She waddled over to Robyn on chunky legs, handing it to her with a toothless smile of encouragement.

"Hopefully, this will ease your discomfort some," Mrs. Gingerich offered.

Robyn took a large swallow of the minty, bitter tea. She grimaced at the taste and its lukewarm temperature. "You should add some sugar, Ada Mae. It really is awful."

Ada Mae chuckled. "It isn't supposed to be a treat. Its medicinal properties give it that foul taste. But I've added enough peppermint to mask it a little."

Robyn reluctantly nodded in agreement, then tilted her head. "Shhh," she shushed the others with a finger to her lips, listening. "A buggy approaches."

Ada Mae rushed to the window, pushing the white gossamer curtains aside. "It's Jonas. He made it in time."

The next contraction that rocked Robyn didn't bother her as much as the previous ones. After eighteen years of marriage, she still experienced the fluttering of butterflies whenever Jonas returned from a day away. This would probably be their last child. At forty-one, Robyn was feeling too worn out to go through another pregnancy, labor and suckling babe. Jonas had been surprised to learn about this pregnancy. Verna, their last child, was nearly seven years old, but he didn't know that Robyn had been taking primrose oil in hopes of conceiving one last time. She was trying for that little boy they'd wanted since their first pregnancy so many years earlier.

Robyn already had the crushing feeling that this child was, in fact, another girl. Until the baby was born, she'd keep hoping and praying for that special boy. When Jonas had laid his hands on her belly months ago, he'd proclaimed that they were indeed having a girl. Until then, and delivering more than a hundred babies in this community and the surrounding ones, he'd never been wrong. Even with the odds stacked against her, she'd keep faith that maybe he had finally made a mistake. In case he had, she'd already picked out the boy's name. Simon Levi Peachey. If it turned out to be a girl, Esta.

Robyn would love the child either way, but she couldn't lie, even to herself. A fifth girl would be disappointing.

The faint sound of her youngest daughters, Gloria and Verna, shrieking downstairs met Robyn's ears. She almost didn't notice the beginning of another contraction as she stared at the door, waiting impatiently for Jonas to burst in.

When the door flung open, Robyn caught a glimpse of the girls peeking in before Mrs. Gingerich scurried over to close it, blocking her daughters' view. Childbirth wasn't pleasant to witness, especially for children. They were too young to understand the pain and suffering their momma had to endure. Later, after the blood and mess were cleaned up, and the soiled sheets were removed from the room, the girls would meet their newest sibling, but not a moment before.

Jonas lifted the black hat from his head, tossing it on the dresser beside the door. His clear blue eyes were calm and the corner of his mouth lifted into a half-smile. A few gray hairs mingled with the brown ones in the thick beard that ran down the length of his chest. Those gray hairs were the only visible proof of his thirty-eight years. There was a youthful, charismatic quality about Jonas that made everyone like the medicine man. As a teen, he'd been one of the most sought after boys in the community. A shy, blonde girl named Robyn had ultimately won his favor.

He nodded at Mrs. Gingerich first and then his sister before he turned his attention to Robyn. "How are you fairing, wife?" He had the gift of a steady voice no matter the circumstance. Robyn loved that voice. Hearing it, she relaxed.

"It goes difficult this time. Ada Mae had me pushing earlier, but the child is taking its sweet time," Robyn drawled the words, reaching for her husband's hand.

Jonas pulled his suspenders from his shoulders. He knelt beside the bed, taking Robyn's hand and pressing it to the side of his face. "Rest assured, I am here now," he told Robyn before glancing at Ada Mae with a frown. "You should have waited for me. I deliver all the children in these parts, especially my own."

Ada Mae's green eyes flicked from Robyn to Jonas. She shrugged. "You of all people should know sometimes babies don't wait for anyone."

As if he was used to such insolence from his younger sister, he sighed and rose to his feet.

Ignoring Ada Mae's comment, he asked, "Do you have everything prepared?"

"Of course. Don't I always?" Ada Mae huffed.

"Yes, I suppose you do," he replied in a tired voice.

He rolled up his sleeves and dipped his hands into the sudsy water in the washbasin. Mrs. Gingerich handed him a towel before she busied herself plumping the pillows behind Robyn.

Ada Mae brought a wooden tray with raised handles to Jonas. It contained everything from scissors and thread to cloths and iodine, arranged neatly. There were several dark glass bottles filled with herb mixtures, essential oils and tinctures.

Jonas plucked one of the bottles from the tray and poured it into a small cup. "Here, drink this. It will take away the pain and tedium of this delivery," he coaxed, placing the cup into Robyn's hands.

"Oh must I, Jonas? I want to be awake when this one arrives," she said with the wilted tone of disappointment.

Jonas met his wife's pained eyes. "There is no reason for you to suffer so. Have faith in me. It will be over soon."

Robyn glanced at Mrs. Gingerich, who gazed back at her with tight lips and wide eyes. The old woman wouldn't question her husband's ways. He was well known as a miraculous healer. Robyn understood. Then she looked at Ada Mae. Her sister-in-law graced her with a firm shake of her head and a slight smile.

Robyn swallowed the contents of the cup down resignedly. Who was she or anyone else for that matter to question Jonas Peachey?

The liquid burned as it slid down her throat. She closed her eyes, easing back into the pillows. Another contraction gripped her insides. The pain was still there, but it was numbed, distant feeling, and so were the voices in the room. She strained to listen, catching Jonas' quiet, yet commanding voice as he said a short prayer for the health of her and their baby. He called out orders to Ada Mae and Mrs. Gingerich in quick succession.

The sound of the words and the shuffling of feet on the hardwood floor drifted away. Robyn was at peace. When she felt the pressure of hands pushing down on her belly and pull-ing within her womb, she didn't startle.

Her mind wandered. She thought about the lavender dress she had almost finished sewing for Verna and how she might allow the child to work the final stitches on the hem herself. She wouldn't have much time to do it herself. She'd be busy in the coming days with a new baby. She hadn't even completed the crib quilt yet. She'd been waiting to see whether it was a boy or a girl before picking the trim color.

Dear Lord, please make it so Jonas is wrong. Give me a baby boy, Robyn prayed, as the world went dark and quiet.

1

SERENITY

March 24, 2015
Blood Rock Amish Settlement, Indiana

"Here we go again." Todd Roftin gave an exaggerated roll of his brown eyes.

I couldn't help sighing myself as I slid into the front passenger seat of the cruiser. As usual, Todd was driving. Bobby Humphrey, the county coroner and all around go-to guy for forensic questions, took the back seat.

I regretted ordering the double bacon cheeseburger from Nancy's Diner. It felt like a heavy rock rested in my gut. The little burp that escaped didn't relieve the bloated feeling.

"You eat too much greasy food, Serenity. Your arteries are probably already clogged," Todd informed me with a sideways sneer.

"You should talk," I fired back. I wasn't in the mood for sparing with Todd and indigestion was only part of the reason. "For every burger I eat at Nancy's, you eat two."

"Yeah, but at least I have Heather back at the house cooking some decent meals during the week. Do you even cook?" Todd raised a brow.

Bobby snorted. I ignored him.

"I make do just fine in that department, thank you very much. I know all about Heather's cooking skills. I've eaten at your house enough times to know that her meals aren't that much different from what we eat at the diner."

Todd opened his mouth to protest when Bobby promptly shut him up.

"Don't you think we should focus on the call that just came in and not worry so much about everyone's eating habits? I swear the two of you are more like squabbling siblings than the sheriff and deputy of Blood Rock."

I glanced over my shoulder and forced a smile. Bobby should have retired by now, but he loved his job, despite his constant complains. I figured that spending all day, every day, with his wife was a lot worse than working full time with dead bodies. I wouldn't say it out loud, but I was glad for his troubles at home. I couldn't imagine what I'd do without the grumpy wisdom he dispensed on a daily basis.

"The death of a woman while having a home birth doesn't sound like sheriff's business to me." I shrugged, facing forward.

The argument I'd had with Daniel that morning had my stomach rolling more than the burger. His stubborn ways had flared up again. The last thing I wanted to deal with on this cloudy afternoon was Amish intrigue.

"That's not exactly what Bishop Aaron Esch said on the phone..." Todd trailed off when I flashed him a withering look.

"Amish drama. That's all this is." I made a cutting motion with my hand to signal the end of the conversation.

The historic brick buildings, neat sidewalks and ornate street lamps disappeared as we left the city limits. The trees beyond the car's windows still had the fluffy, yellowish look of budding leaves. The fields were plowed and miles of dark, churned earth spread out on either side of the road. Yellow flashes of daffodils and forsythia bushes began as we passed farmsteads.

The improved weather was the only thing that kept my foul mood in check. It was difficult to be grouchy when the snow had finally melted and birds were chirping. I rolled down the window a few more inches and tilted my face to the rush of warm air. Every year, the first spring days in Indiana felt heaven sent. It was a relief to be at winter's end.

"What do you make of it, Bobby?" I reluctantly asked.

My last meeting with the bishop was still fresh on my mind. Two months earlier, when I'd gotten back from my insane trip up north to help with the arson investigation in the Poplar Springs' Amish settlement, Bishop Esch had stopped by my office to complain about the arrival of a new family. I'd listened to the bishop talk about vague healing practices that sometimes went awry. He'd given no specifics. No crimes had been committed as far as I could tell. I'd sent the tall, elderly man on his way, explaining as best as I could that law enforcement couldn't arrest someone who hadn't committed a crime. We weren't in the business of running people out of town, either.

"From what Aaron said, the young woman was hiding her pregnancy from her family and the rest of the community. She was only midway into her second trimester. It seems she died while having a miscarriage, which is not very common, I might add," Bobby said.

I continued to gaze out the window at the newly mint-green world, frowning. I certainly wasn't an expert on pregnancy. Maybe Bobby was on to something.

"Is the bishop implying that her death is a homicide?" I asked. A quick glance at Todd showed his expression was grim.

Without looking back at Bobby, I knew he was twirling the end of his mustache whiskers between his fingers. When he spoke, he sounded cautious.

"That's the feeling I got from the man. We won't rush to judgment on the matter until I conduct the autopsy."

"It doesn't make sense. In Naomi Beiler's case, the bishop wanted nothing more than to cover up the entire incident so that he could resolve the issue vigilante style. Now he's begging for our help with a matter that probably isn't even criminal," I said, hoping that Bobby would see my aversion to getting involved.

"Maybe Aaron Esch is afraid," Todd muttered.

I leaned over. "Afraid of what?"

Todd's shrug made the back of my neck tingle. "Sounds like voodoo shit to me," Todd replied. "I watched this show a while back about a crazy medicine woman in Haiti who was taking out her enemies in this fishing town. They were just dropping one after the other, for no apparent reason."

"I'm sure that most of those deaths can be attributed to poisons of some kind. There is also a theory about the mind's ability to cause damage to the body when a person truly believes they've had a curse put on them," Bobby added.

I held up my hand. "Whoa. We're talking about the Amish here, not some superstitious witchcraft religion on an island." I scoffed.

"Voodoo isn't what you think it is. I've spent some time over the years studying foreign cultures. For the most part, it's a spiritual religion, comprised of a type of folk magic." Bobby rested his arms over the front seat.

I turned to him. "Do you really believe there's magic involved in any of these cult practices."

He shrugged, settling back into his seat. "Not everything can be proven or understood by science."

"I agree. Have you heard about those people who spontaneously burst into flames? I watched a special about it the other night…"

I blocked Todd's ramblings and stared out the window. Among the mostly bare branches in the groves we passed were clusters of pinkish-purplish flowers. I caught a scent of blossoms on the breeze and inhaled. The grass bursting from the earth was such a lush green it almost looked fake.

"Here's the place." Bobby pointed his bony finger between Todd and me.

Jeremy's cruiser and an ambulance were parked beside a small, white farmhouse. Four buggies were already lined up on the gravel driveway.

Thudding my head against the headrest, I grumbled, "It never ceases to amaze me how quickly the Amish show up when something bad happens. This must be the closest thing to a TV show they have."

"What has you in such a foul mood?" Bobby clucked his tongue. "A young woman has died. Adjust your attitude to the circumstances," he ordered.

I overlooked Todd's smirking face. Bobby was right. I was being a bitch. And it wasn't just about Daniel. A couple of months earlier, I'd shot a man named Asher Schwartz. He'd deserved it and I wasn't suffering remorse over his death, but another innocent person had died on my watch. The image of Jotham Hochstetler bleeding out on the Amish schoolhouse floor was seared into my consciousness, like Naomi's pale and lifeless form in the cornfield. Over time, a cop became desensitized to cruelty and death, but for me, the pictures didn't go away.

I took a measured breath and straightened my sunglasses, putting on my best game face. "What's the woman's name?"

"Fannie Kuhns. Twenty-one years old," Bobby said.

As Todd parked the car, my eyes skimmed the crowd of darkly clad people gathered in front of the house. I spotted the tall silhouette of Bishop Aaron Esch and the round one of James Hooley, one of the ministers. Moses Bachman, Daniel's father, was with them, along with several other long-bearded Amish men I recognized and a couple I didn't.

I couldn't stop my heart from racing. Walking into a group of stoic Amish men gave me the creeps and this particular group was worse. They'd held me prisoner in a barn not so long ago. It was fine to forgive, but forgetting something like that was foolish. I'd learned long ago that the Amish weren't the pacifist people I'd assumed they were. Reality checks sucked.

Daniel walked out through the front door behind his mother and I knew my day was completely shot to hell.

"What's the boyfriend doing here?" Todd's lips twisted.

"He used to be Amish and his entire family still is. It's not so strange for him to be present," I said as convincingly as I could. Inside though, I was wondering the same thing.

The three of us were making our way across the yard when the front door opened again. This time, EMPs exited the house with a gurney.

"Dammit," I muttered under my breath, breaking into a jog. Todd and Bobby followed on my heels. Bobby huffed at the exertion and Todd's keys jingled on his belt.

The crowd split to allow us to pass through. I caught a glimpse of the bishop and James Hooley joining the back of our parade up the porch steps. The pots filled with pansies on each side of the doorway made the young woman's death seem more surreal than it already did.

"Why did you move the body?" I demanded of Raymond, at the front of the gurney. Lucky for Beth, she was at the back.

Raymond's eyes rounded and his slender face flushed. He was tall, gangly and a bit awkward at times. Beth was a firecracker.

"I didn't know there was any kind of investigation planned." Raymond thumbed over his shoulder. "Jeremy gave us the go ahead to bag her."

"That's right," Beth added from the house. Jeremy was further back in the room, talking to a teary-eyed, older woman and a much younger one, who stared ahead in shock.

I inwardly groaned. I hated dealing with grieving families. It was impossible to be respectful of their loss and ask nosy questions.

I risked a glance at Daniel, leaning back against the porch railing. When our eyes met, he smiled.

It was annoying how a million butterflies took flight in my stomach like I was a sixteen-year-old school girl. I swallowed. *I'm thirty-four and way too old for weak knees in the presence of a man. Even a tall, well-muscled and handsome one like Daniel.*

"So. How long have you been here?" I asked.

Daniel shrugged and glanced at his mother. The two weren't close, so their being together was intriguing in itself.

Anna spoke quietly to Daniel in the Pennsylvania-German dialect of the Amish. I had no idea what they were saying, but I didn't need to understand. Anna didn't take her eyes off me while she talked, and I was good at reading voice fluctuations and body language. She was disturbed, and not in a grieving way, either.

Daniel turned back to me. "About ten minutes. Fannie Kuhns was my mother's niece and my cousin." He paused as if deciding whether to say more. The tension on the porch was palpable. Todd stood quietly beside me, and Bobby whispered back and forth with Beth. I could hear the scribbling of his pencil in his notebook. I was too distracted to catch everything, but the gist was that Bobby wanted basic information about the state and location of the body without having to open the zipper in front of the entire community.

"Ah, my father contacted me this morning. He had something important to talk about." He shook his head at my questioning eyes. "This isn't a good place to discuss it. I'll tell you everything later."

"We don't have the luxury of waiting for this conversation. It needs to be taken care of now," Bishop Esch announced, stepping onto the porch. He stopped in front of me and pointed into the crowd. "You must arrest that man."

Several of the Amish men moved aside, leaving one standing alone.

I stared at the man. He was tall, straight-backed and smirking slightly. There was a sprinkling of gray at his temples. The rest of the brown hair poking out from under his hat was curly. His beard was long and thick. The top few buttons of his ivory shirt were unbuttoned. His boots weren't muddy like the other men. The oddest and most mesmerizing part about the man were his eyes. They were the lightest blue I'd ever seen.

When the man returned my gaze, his mouth loosened into a friendly smile. My heart rate sped up and the breath caught in my throat.

This must be the medicine man.

2

DANIEL

S eeing Jonas Peachey sent a shiver up my spine. The healing man had always given me the creeps, even though I'd only seen him a few times as a child. I still remembered the threatening glint in his eyes when Aaron Esch had questioned him about his healing practices following the unexpected death of an elderly man suffering the final stages of cancer. My family was visiting relatives in the Black Willow Amish settlement when it had happened. Aaron had been there at the same time visiting his sister, Robyn, Jonas' wife.

The look Jonas had given Aaron for questioning his tactics and authority in that Ohio community was odd for an Amish man. I'd only been about ten at the time, but I'd recognized it for what it was. Jonas believed the only authority he answered to was himself. He'd told Aaron that perhaps the old man had wanted death. The implication of his words still made my heart pound.

I shook away the memory and glanced at Serenity.

Her blonde hair was pulled back in its usual ponytail, and the large aviator sunglasses she wore covered a fair amount of her face. Her plump lips were pursed as she stared at Jonas. Physical longing stirred in my groin. I wished I'd kissed her goodbye earlier, instead of wasting a perfectly good morning arguing.

Between a suspicious death in the community and the suspected involvement of the mysterious Jonas Peachey, there wouldn't be any time for romance.

"May I speak with you alone, Bishop Esch?" Serenity asked.

When Aaron nodded, Serenity turned back to Jonas. "You should stick around. I have a few questions for you, too."

Serenity murmured a few words to the paramedics and Bobby before she allowed Fannie Kuhn's body to be taken from the house. When she went inside, Aaron, Bobby and Todd followed her.

I glanced at Ma.

"Tell the Sheriff what I've told you," she said before she hurried down the steps to my waiting father. He shook his head when his eyes met mine.

I took my own worried breath when I entered the house. Serenity was talking quietly to Irene Kuhns, Fannie's mother, while a young woman I assumed was Fannie's sister looked on with a puffy, red face. Aaron and Bobby sat a discreet distance away at the kitchen table, talking quietly. Bobby scribbled in his notebook the entire time.

Todd sidled up to me. With a raised brow, he whispered, "What the hell's going on around here?"

I couldn't help smiling at his blunt words. I was thinking the same, but wouldn't have dared say so. That was Todd's way. He couldn't be subtle if his life depended on it.

I shrugged. "I guess that's what we're going to have to find out."

Todd rubbed the bristle on his chin. "You should ask Serenity to add you to the payroll. You're working enough cases with us."

I snorted. "Don't think it hasn't already occurred to me."

"Bobby, Daniel," Serenity said, jerking her chin at us to join her.

I didn't hesitate, crossing the room quicker than Bobby. I didn't know Irene well, but I remembered her from my childhood in the community. She was one of the milder women, about fifteen years younger than my mother and extremely shy around outsiders. Seeing the tears dribble down her round cheeks made me uncomfortable. The woman's grief was like a water-filled balloon ready to explode. It physically pushed at me, making me take a step back and glance away.

The younger woman had the same plump, roundish features and strawberry blonde hair as Irene. Her tight face said she struggled to keep the tears in.

When Bobby reached us, Serenity took a tea cup from Irene. She held out the cup to Bobby, who pulled a pair of latex gloves from his pocket and put them on before he touched it.

"The contents of the cup were the last and only thing Fannie ingested today. It's empty, but it hasn't been washed. Can you get any forensics from it?" Serenity asked.

Bobby nodded slowly. "I can swab the interior and send it off to the state lab. There might be enough residue to get a list of some of the ingredients, but with trace evidence, I doubt anything we find will be sufficient to hold up in court." He brought the cup to his nose and inhaled, then looked at Irene. "Peppermint?"

"Yes," she confirmed. "It makes the parsley tea taste better."

"Did you know your daughter was pregnant?" Bobby asked.

Irene glanced at her daughter. The girl squeezed her mother's hand in encouragement before Irene responded.

"I learned of it just today when Fannie began bleeding." Irene gulped and licked her lips. Tears welled in her eyes.

"I'm sorry. I know this is difficult, but it's really best to talk about what happened while it's still fresh in your mind. We all want to know what happened to Fannie," Serenity coaxed.

Irene sucked in a wet breath and dabbed her eyes with her apron. When she collected herself, she nodded.

Serenity faced the daughter. "How long have you known about your sister's condition?"

With Serenity's sunglasses pushed up on top of her head, her eyes were visible. There was a hint of accusation in those dark blue eyes. Serenity had a knack for reading people. I guessed she'd pegged the sister's prior knowledge of the pregnancy accurately.

The girl didn't look at her mother. She swallowed and replied, "I suspected it for the past couple of weeks."

"What's your name?" Serenity's pen was poised above the small notebook in her hand.

"Hannah—Hannah Kuhns."

"I'm sure this is very upsetting for you to talk about right after your sister's death." Serenity hesitated. "Was Fannie married?"

Before Hannah could answer, Irene shook her head, pulling her apron up to her face. "I can't do this right now," she mumbled, hurrying from the room. Her footsteps on the staircase boomed throughout the house.

Serenity didn't miss a beat. "Where's your father?"

"He died three years ago," Hannah said, the words so soft I had to lean forward to hear.

"How old are you?"

"Eighteen."

Serenity's face relaxed. Hannah wasn't a minor. Serenity could continue to question her without her mother's presence.

"It's really important that we know who the father of the baby is." Serenity lowered her voice. "Do you have any idea who it might be?"

Hannah's eyes widened. While she hesitated, I held my breath. I had the feeling Serenity and Bobby were, too.

"No, I don't," Hannah said. "May I go now?"

I looked at Serenity. She didn't immediately answer. Her face was still as she considered, then she gave a curt nod. "You may. I don't expect you're planning a trip or anything. I'll need to talk to you again once your sister is laid to rest."

"And her baby. The child must be buried, too," Hannah said.

"Of course. When both of them are buried."

Hannah whirled away, trotting up the steps after her mother.

Serenity scowled at me and Bobby. We took a step closer together as Todd joined our group. "Are you kidding me?" Serenity whispered.

"As I've told you before, nothing is simple or straightforward with the Amish," Bobby said, tilting his head. He twirled the end of his gray mustache between his fingers.

Serenity lifted her hand and pointed to her fingers as she talked. "We have a young pregnant woman. She's not married. She dies under somewhat strange circumstances and her family doesn't want to talk about it." Her gaze settled on me. "Sound familiar?"

"Maybe she died of natural causes." I paused to look at Bobby. "It happens sometimes, doesn't it?"

Bobby nodded. "Sure it does. If the pregnancy develops somewhere other than the uterus, a rupture can occur that causes internal bleeding and death, but that usually happens much earlier in a pregnancy. Beth indicated that the fetus looked to be around four months along. It's odd that a catastrophic event would take place at that point in the pregnancy."

"What if something like this happens to Heather?" Todd interrupted.

We turned to look at him. He was pale and frowning.

Bobby rested his hand on Todd's shoulder. "Heather has been seeing an obstetrician on a regular basis since the very beginning of conception. Trust me, her doctor would know by now if she had any problems with the pregnancy or the baby. She's in good hands." Bobby dismissed him and turned back to Serenity. "Usually, if a mother dies in the process, it's early in the pregnancy or at the end when a full term baby is delivered and there are complications. This woman's death is mystery."

"How long will the autopsy take?" Serenity asked.

"I'll get right on it. I should have some information for you by tomorrow. The state lab's analysis of this cup—" Bobby held it up. "—will take a couple of days with a rush order. I'd be remiss if I didn't mention that parsley tea is a known herbal abortifacient."

"Parsley can cause miscarriage?" Serenity said with wide-eyed disbelief.

"It's a primitive treatment that's been used for centuries to induce menstruation and bleeding," Bobby stressed.

Serenity glanced around the room. Aaron was still seated at the table, but his head was turned toward us. Several women were making their way to the stairway and a small group of men were gathered on the porch beyond the screened door.

"Whoa, wait a minute, ladies," Serenity called out. Todd walked to the front of the line, blocking the staircase. All eyes turned to Serenity. "Jeremy, over here." Serenity motioned to the young deputy.

Jeremy squeezed in between the women. "Yes, ma'am," he said when he reached us.

"Where was the body when you arrived?" Serenity asked.

"Upstairs. She was on a bed," Jeremy replied, blinking.

Serenity looked in Bobby's direction and the old man started toward the stairs. "I'm on it."

Serenity flicked her finger for Todd to join the coroner.

When it was just Serenity, me and Jeremy, she asked, "Where was the fetus?"

"Wrapped in a towel beside the body." Jeremy took a breath. "Raymond and Beth bagged them together."

Serenity sighed. "Get these people out of here. Only family members in the house."

I spoke up. "Ah, Serenity. Everyone here is probably related in one way or another."

Serenity rolled her eyes, but sighed in understanding. "Okay. Only the mother and sister are allowed to stay. Clear the house."

Jeremy hesitated on the balls of his feet. "Is this a murder investigation?"

"I sure hope not, but until we know for sure, we'll treat it like it is," Serenity replied.

When we were alone, Aaron rose from his chair. Serenity held up her hand, stopping him. "Give us a minute, please."

I followed Serenity into the adjoining room. There was a small burgundy couch and two tan chairs in the small space. I glanced back through the open doorway at Jeremy as he herded the Amish women from the house. They argued quietly with him while he ushered them along. I certainly didn't envy his job.

"What do you know about all of this?" Serenity demanded.

Her accusing tone made my stomach clench. So much for, *"Hi dear, how's your day going?"*

"I don't know anything." I threw up my hands.

Serenity wasn't convinced. She leaned in closer, her eyes narrowed. "Why were you here with your mother?"

I drew in a deep breath. Only once before had I felt such strong emotion for a woman and it had been the worst mistake of my life. I couldn't deny that I loved Serenity, but I was still wondering if we'd be together in the end. The damn woman had a solid brick wall around her that I couldn't penetrate no matter how hard I tried. She didn't trust me.

"Father and Ma wanted to talk to me about Jonas Peachey—"

"The medicine man?"

"Yes. He moved into town right about the time we were doing the arson investigation in Poplar Springs."

"Yeah, I know. The bishop paid me a visit early on. He wanted me to run the man and his family off or something. It was weird. He didn't give me any actual reasons for his intense discomfort with Mr. Peachey. He was keeping secrets, as usual." Serenity scoffed.

I didn't know whether to frown or chuckle. Serenity's lips pressed tightly together.

"Why didn't you mention this to me a long time ago?"

Serenity shrugged. "It didn't seem important at the time." She shifted her feet. "I thought it was just Amish drama—nothing the authorities needed to be involved with."

I half-laughed, shaking my head. "Since I used to be Amish and these are my people, it should have occurred to you that I'd be interested. Hell, you should have wanted to share the information with me."

Several emotions passed over Serenity's face. Anger flashed and turned to reluctant contriteness.

"Sorry. I got busy with other things. Can we talk about it now?" Serenity's eyes glittered with hopefulness.

"I guess we have no choice." Serenity's pretty face darkened with hostility and I added, "Ma told me that there have been some strange healing practices going on in the community lately. She was concerned that things might get out of hand. She wanted me to talk to you about it."

"I can't arrest people who haven't committed a crime yet," Serenity pointed out.

"Would it make you more inclined to do so if you knew that Jonas had visited the Kuhns family several times in recent weeks? And that Jonas' wife died in childbirth?"

Serenity pulled her little notebook out of her pocket. "Go on," she said.

3

SERENITY

I stared across the table at Bishop Esch, my mind swirling. "Robyn Peachey, Jonas' wife, was your sister?"

"She was the youngest child in my family. That's why I'm so well acquainted with Jonas," the bishop said.

The Amish man was tall and thin. His long beard was mostly white, as was his hair and his bushy eyebrows. His black hat, coat and pants made him look like the harbinger of death. I still remembered him standing over me as I had lain bleeding and bruised on the dirt floor of the abandoned barn. He was a vigilante leader—a scary guy. But for all that, I'd managed to come to a truce with him, although it was awkward at times.

The bishop leaned further across the table on his elbows. "I was visiting Robyn and her girls at their home in Ohio when she died."

"Was her death similar to this one?" I pointed straight up, indicating where Fannie Kuhns died.

The bishop frowned. "She was in labor when it happened. Her daughter survived."

I glanced at my notes. "The girl would be about ten years old now?"

"Yes, that is correct."

I glanced at my notes. "And your brother-in-law takes care of his two youngest girls, Verna and Esta?"

Bishop Esch shook his head. "Jonas may live in the same house, but it's his sister, Ada Mae, who cares for the children. Always has, since Robyn's death."

My eyes strayed to Daniel as I organized the relationships of everyone we'd been discussing in my mind.

"So. Jonas Peachey came to the Kuhns' home on several occasions to provide medicinal relief to someone this month? That's all you have?"

"Isn't that enough, Sheriff?" His eyebrows rose.

"I'm afraid it's all circumstantial." The bishop slumped in his seat at my words. My gut tightened and I went out on a limb. "Let me interview a few more people and get the autopsy and toxicology reports back." I didn't flinch when I met Bishop Esch's hard gaze. "Don't worry. We'll keep an eye on Jonas."

Daniel and I left the bishop whispering to James Hooley in the corner of the kitchen. There were two groups of people waiting in the yard and Jeremy was standing at the base of the steps, guarding the entrance to the house. To the right were about a dozen men and to the left were the same number of women. Children of all ages sat across the front lawn. They all seemed to be waiting for something to happen. A line of buggies was parked along the driveway.

"Did Bobby and Todd manage to sneak by us while we were talking to the bishop?" I asked Jeremy.

He blew out a sigh of relief at our appearance. The young deputy was an excellent cop, except when dealing with the Amish. He was terrified of them.

"Yes, ma'am." He nodded vigorously. "Bobby told me to tell you that he'd collected everything he needed and that Todd took photos of the room. He'd see you back at the office. He wanted to get started on the autopsy right away."

Daniel nudged my arm and I looked at him. I wasn't exactly short at five foot five, but I always had to crane my neck when I stood too close to Daniel's six five, muscled frame. His dark brown hair curled messily around his head, and his brown eyes were anxious.

"I don't see Jonas Peachey." He continued to search the crowd.

"Jeremy, did the blue-eyed man, the one who the bishop pointed out earlier, slip away?" I asked, drawing out the question, dreading his answer.

Jeremy swallowed, glanced around and looked back at me. "I'm sorry, ma'am. They're all dressed the same and having those beards, I can't tell them apart."

I took a calming breath. I got it, but it annoyed the crap out of me. "They are different when you take the time to really look at them. Some are tall and some are short. They have varying lengths and colors of beards." I paused and motioned at the crowd with my hand. "If you look closely, they're not all wearing coats. Some have blue shirts and others are wearing tan ones. It's not that difficult, and one last thing." Jeremy looked sullenly at me like a dog kicked off the porch. "For the hundredth time, stop calling me ma'am. Serenity will do."

"I'm sorry, ma—Serenity. I will...try." Jeremy stumbled over the words.

I waved him away. "Go ahead and open the house up to the community." I turned back to Daniel. "Do you have any idea where Jonas Peachey's farm is?"

"I sure do." Daniel grinned.

As I followed Daniel's springy step to his Jeep, I got the distinct feeling that he was excited about a brand new mystery to solve.

I hoped that it would keep him preoccupied and we wouldn't have to continue our conversation from this morning any time soon.

ᘒ

"How well do you know this guy?" I asked, gazing out the window at the neat farmhouses and the dark earth of the cropland surrounding them.

The sun was all but gone and with the cloudy, darkening sky came the strong scent of dampness on the cooler air. I kept my sunglasses on anyway. I didn't want Daniel to read my thoughts through my eyes.

"I met him on a few occasions when I was a kid. Robyn is a distant cousin of mine. To the Amish, cousins are as important as siblings, even if they're second cousins once removed. I spent a lot of time when I was growing up traveling around from one Amish settlement to another to see my parents' extended family."

"What did you think of him back then?" I tilted my head sideways to study Daniel's profile. His nose was strong and straight. His sunglasses kept me from reading him as well.

"Honestly, the man scared me. He has real powers."

"Powers? Can you elaborate?" I couldn't keep the pitch of my voice from rising at the absurdity of the conversation.

Daniel chuckled. "All right. I know this probably sounds crazy to a scientific-minded person like yourself, but there are people who are gifted with the ability to heal others."

When I grunted, he hurried on, "Now wait a minute. My mother has been blessed that way. Granted, her powers aren't as strong as Jonas', but she's healed before."

"Are you serious? You don't really believe in all that charlatan nonsense."

"I've seen it with my own eyes," Daniel said, smacking his hand on the wheel. "When I was around eight years old, I was riding double with my friend Lester Lapp—Mervin's father—on a newly broke colt. I didn't realize the maple tree we'd stopped beneath had a hornet's nest in it. When we heard the buzzing, it was too late. The stings on my neck and arms weren't nearly as bad as when that colt went into a bucking fit. We fell off and Lester hit the tree. Ma heard our screams and came running from the house. I was already up and had dragged Lester away from the tree and the bees, but he wasn't moving. Blood was mixed in with his blond hair." Daniel took a deep breath and shook the memory loose before he continued. "I'll never forget how I held my breath while Ma laid her hands on Lester. She was murmuring that he was still with us—that he hadn't left his body yet. Then she began praying. They weren't ordinary words coming from her mouth, not entirely German or English. It was a language that I'd never heard before. Her eyes glazed over and her words turned into a constant stream of strange mumblings. The wind picked up around us and

I began moving my own mouth, praying to God not to take my best friend away.

"A moment later, Ma fell over and I moved around Lester's prone body to reach her. She was asleep. That's when Lester opened his eyes and asked what happened. Ma slept a lot the rest of the week. She wouldn't talk about the incident in front of us kids."

My heart was racing by the time he stopped talking, but I didn't want to believe. "In hindsight, don't you think that maybe Lester was simply unconscious from the fall and he woke up naturally?"

"What about Ma?" Daniel asked.

"Maybe some kind of induced hysteria, I don't know. It's easier to believe that she lost her mind for a moment than she actually used supernatural powers to heal Lester."

"There are things in this world that can't be explained. I know what I saw and what I felt. It was real," Daniel said with sureness before he turned onto the winding gravel driveway that led up a hill to a blue farmhouse with a wraparound porch. Most Amish homes were white. Seeing the different color set the immediate tone that these weren't ordinary Amish people.

"All that aside, if Jonas is supposed to have healing powers, why would he use those gifts to harm people?"

"That's what we're going to have to figure out. Healers don't always just use their own bodily forces to cure people. Oftentimes, it's their knowledge of herbs and different plants that give them the ability to make teas, oils, tinctures and poultices that do the healing. This kind of knowledge is passed down from generation to generation and is more powerful than even the *laying of the hands,* sometimes.

I absorbed his words as he parked the Jeep and turned off the engine. When he looked at me, he was frowning.

"Be careful with Jonas. Even if you don't believe that he has powers, he is crafty. Keep your guard up the entire time you're around him, and for heaven's sake, don't—"

"Drink or eat anything," I cut him off, smirking.

"I'm not kidding," Daniel said with a sterner voice.

I couldn't resist. I leaned in and kissed his lips. At first they were stubbornly unresponsive, but when my tongue tried to push them apart, they loosened and opened hungrily. This part of our relationship was more than okay. It was his pestering about other things that gave me fits.

A thought occurred and I pulled back. He groaned, but released me.

"If Jonas Peachey is so scary, then how does he get any business?"

Daniel chuckled as if I were either stupid or naïve. I bristled.

"He may be a strange man, but he has a gift. If your child were sick, wouldn't you do anything to save him or her? Besides, you'll see for yourself. He's a charmer."

All I could reply was a weak, "Maybe," as I clutched the door handle and stepped out.

"Are you ready?" I asked with deliberate slowness.

Daniel met my gaze and smiled. "I'm fine. You're the one who has no idea what you're getting yourself into."

A shiver passed through me. I wouldn't say it out loud, but I was afraid he was right.

4

SERENITY

S cented candles burned on the fireplace mantle, and dim light shone through the small windows. I sat beside Daniel on an uncomfortable Shaker style wooden bench and across from Ada Mae. It was hard to tell her age at a glance. The hair poking out from beneath her white cap was auburn and her eyes were green. She was slender and straight backed, but like other middle-aged Amish women, the gray hairs at her temples weren't colored. Her oval face was make-up free, exposing a few discolorations and wrinkles. The resemblance to her brother made me squirm. They shared the same sculptured high cheekbones, straight noses and slant at the corner of their eyes. Her wandering eyes told me she had a busy mind. She was more composed than I expected her to be, almost as if she'd been expecting our visit.

"Are you sure you don't want a cup of coffee or tea?" she repeated.

"No, we're fine. Thank you, though." I caught the raise of her brows and added, "What brought you and your family here to Blood Rock?"

Ada Mae smiled and stared out the window. The tapping of light rain on the tin roof was a soft, constant drone. The sound made me sleepy.

"Jonas was guided to come here by a dream," she said in a faraway, quiet voice. She continued to gaze out the rain-streaked window.

I glanced at Daniel. He shrugged, looking uncomfortable.

"Those dried plants hanging over there. What are they?" I motioned to the bundles dangling from the rafter.

Ada Mae's face brightened when she turned back. She stood and crossed the room, telling me what they were. "Lavender…St. John's wart, valerian root…and ginseng."

"What do you use those particular plants for?" I asked.

Ada Mae's voice became more animated as she talked. "Of course the lavender is used for its wonderful scent, but it also has calming effects, like chamomile. Valerian root can help a person sleep better, but brings vivid dreams. St. John's wart is used as an anti-inflammatory and soothes a depressed spirit. I primarily use ginseng to fight infections, but it has many other benefits."

"Did your brother teach you about herbs and their uses?"

She smiled. "No. It was my grandmother who taught me the healing arts." She shrugged. "Of course it was Jonas who inherited Grandmother's healing touch, not me."

It wasn't resentment I sensed in her tone, more wistfulness.

I was about to question Ada Mae more about the *healing touch* when a teenager burst into the room. She looked strikingly similar to Jonas, from her dark hair to her faint blue eyes. I scanned my notes and guessed the girl to be Verna.

"Mervin is tying up his horse right…" The girl's voice trailed off and she blushed when she saw me and Daniel.

Ada Mae chuckled. "Verna, this is Sheriff Adams and Daniel Bachman. They are here to see your Da."

Verna recovered and nodded her head in my direction. She didn't look at Daniel, dropping her eyes when they passed over him. "Sorry. I didn't know we had company." She giggled into her hand. "Your car must be parked on the other side of the house."

"Yes, that's correct," I said, stepping forward. I held out my hand to the girl. She looked surprised at the gesture, but grasped it in a firm grip anyway.

The light rap on the door turned all of our heads. A man called out in the Amish language. The only words I recognized were "Hullo" and "Lester Lapp."

"Come in, Lester," Ada Mae called out in English for my benefit.

Lester walked through the door with his teenage son, Mervin. Daniel greeted Lester with a combined handshake and backslap. He squeezed Mervin's shoulder and they chatted in their native language. The names Fannie and Irene popped up between the unintelligible words in their conversation.

"I take it Mr. Bachman and Lester know each other?" Ada Mae inclined her head. The lines at the corners of her eyes crinkled as she smiled. She leaned in closer, covering the side of her mouth with her hand. "Men are as bad as chickens in a henhouse when they become reacquainted," she whispered.

I smiled in return, but was too absorbed with a quick succession of dark thoughts to agree with Ada Mae. The last time I'd seen Mervin, he'd been sitting in a weathered deer hunting stand. He had held a shotgun and was contemplating suicide. If Daniel and I hadn't shown up when we did and talked him down, he might be dead. The kid had watched his older brother gun down Naomi in a cornfield. Making it worse, Mervin had a crush on her while she was alive. His mother had forced him to keep silent on the matter. It had been my first murder investigation as sheriff in Blood Rock, and my first real interaction with the Amish people.

The other thing on my mind was Daniel's story about his childhood friend being miraculously healed by his mother. This was the same Lester who had supposedly been brought back from near death.

"Serenity, you remember Lester and his son Mervin?" Daniel's voice burst into my thoughts. His question was out of politeness. He knew I wasn't likely to forget the Lapp family.

"Yes, of course." I grasped Lester's hand. "What are you up to these days?"

I tried to keep the sarcasm from my voice, mostly for Mervin's benefit, but I doubted that I was successful.

"Mervin and I are keeping busy getting the fields ready for planting." Lester smiled proudly at his son, then hesitated. "Esther is struggling these days. She visited David at the prison last week. It's hard, you know?"

My contemptuous thoughts softened at Lester's words and his uneasy frown. It took a brave man to talk about a son who had killed a girl, especially one serving life in prison for the crime, but life had to go on for the rest of the family.

Wanting desperately to change the subject, I said, "What brings you here?"

Lester's face brightened. "Do you remember Mervin's leg injury? Jonas and Ada Mae have been healing him. His limp is nearly gone. Tonight is supposed to be his last visit."

"Will Jonas do the laying of his hands?" Daniel asked, reading my thoughts.

Lester nodded, but it was Ada Mae who answered. "I've been treating Mervin with a comfrey paste to aid in his healing, but it hasn't been enough. Jonas will finish the job."

When she said *finish the job* my heart rate sped up. I glanced at Mervin. He'd grown a few inches over the winter and was now taller than me. His blond hair had darkened a shade and most of his freckles were gone. His green eyes were still vibrant, though. Those eyes were so busy staring at Verna, he didn't even notice my appraisal. It abruptly occurred to me why Verna had rushed into the house to announce Mervin's arrival, and why her aunt Ada Mae had laughed.

I was too cynical to get warm, fuzzy feelings about young love. I had experienced my own with Denton McAllister and that single experience had made me a jaded woman. I was happy that Mervin had found some semblance of happiness in his troubled existence. He deserved a break. It was too bad he had to take a liking to this particular girl. If the bishop was correct about Jonas Peachey, the family might not be in Blood Rock for long.

"Do you mind if we stick around for it?" I was skeptical about the magical healing process, but I was also worried about Mervin and what might happen to him if I left him in the medicine man's clutches.

From the corner of my eye, I caught Daniel's firm nod.

"Uh, I don't know about that," Ada Mae said carefully. "First, Lester would have to agree—"

"It's fine with me, Ada. They are friends," Lester interrupted.

I raised my brows at his use of *friends*, but didn't say anything. I looked hopefully back at Ada Mae.

"It will be up to Jonas then," she said.

"What will be up to me?"

The deep voice behind us made my stomach do a somersault. When I turned around, Jonas stood in the doorway. His sharp, tan features were relaxed as if he didn't have a care in the world, but his piercing blue eyes were sharp, and they focused on me.

I walked forward, holding out my hand. "You must be Jonas Peachey. It's nice to finally meet you," I said, connecting with his raised brow gaze. "Of course, if you'd stayed put at the Kuhn's farm, I wouldn't have had to visit your own home."

He grasped my hand. "Sorry about that. I had an errand to run. I've heard some intriguing tales about Blood Rock's sheriff." He smiled. "Though I must admit, I wasn't expecting you to be so young."

I was usually too preoccupied to pick up the subtleties of flirting, but I wasn't completely ignorant about the signs, either. It made my skin crawl to even acknowledge it in my head. This Amish guy was appraising me, but he was smart enough to stay within the boundaries of acceptable behavior, even for an Amish man. I hadn't expected the medicine man to be a Casanova. The realization threw me off balance.

"I hope the stories didn't portray me in a bad light."

"On the contrary. Most folk around here hold you in high esteem." His eyes flicked to Daniel. "You must be Mo's son—the rebellious one. You could be his twin from thirty years ago."

Jonas forgot me as he turned his attention to Daniel. The two men shook hands.

"Yes, I am. I'm surprised you remember me at all. It's been a long time."

"I never forget a face. It's one of my gifts." His attention flicked back to me as he smiled again. "I understand you have some questions for me?"

"Ah, yes, I do, but that can wait." I jutted my chin towards Mervin. "I understand you have a patient to see. I was hoping to sit in on the healing. That is, if it doesn't mess up your mojo or anything."

Jonas glanced at Lester and Ada Mae. "It's fine with me as long as everyone else is comfortable with it."

Lester didn't hesitate. "I have no problem with them observing."

Ada Mae nodded as an answer, then busied herself alongside Verna. Together, they raised a wooden folding table.

Daniel ushered me to the high-backed chairs in the corner where we had a view of the room without being in anyone's way. Butterflies danced in my stomach as Mervin climbed onto the uncomfortable looking table. When he crossed the room, I noticed his limp had lessened considerably from the last time I'd seen him, but he flinched in pain as he walked. I wondered how much of his recovery was related to the passage of time and how much had been affected by the ministrations of Ada Mae.

"You wouldn't believe a miracle if you saw it with your own eyes," Daniel whispered.

When I looked at him, he grinned slightly, but his eyes were troubled. I wasn't sure if he was worried about Mervin or my soul. The thought made me bristle, although I tried not to let him see it.

"If healing can be done magically, then why are there so many people dying of cancer, heart disease and any number of other ailments? There's rarely an easy solution to anything, especially when it comes to medicine," I whispered, continuing to watch the goings-on in the room.

Mervin's eyes were closed. He breathed evenly, but his booted feet tapped together. Verna held out a bowl of something to Jonas. He dipped his hands into the bowl, and rubbed them together.

Ada Mae handed him a towel when he lifted his hands. As if she read my mind, she glanced my way and said, "It's a special oil we use to prepare the hands for healing. There's wood betony, blood root and a few other ingredients in it."

I inhaled, trying to catch the scent of the mixture. All I smelled were the lavender scented flickering candles.

A gust of wind blew in through the windows, flapping the curtains high and extinguishing several of the candles. Ada Mae rushed over to the windows and closed them. The sky outside turned an ominous gray. A flash of lightning zigzagged in the distance. Thunder rumbled and I shivered. Daniel's strong arm went around my shoulder. I didn't shrug him off. I leaned against him, allowing his warmth to chase away the unreasonable chills that came over me.

"Don't let your mind wander too much. You need to stay focused. Ma always told me a distracted mind was a vulnerable one," Daniel whispered.

Was he kidding? I glanced up. He stared ahead, frowning, and I thought, *Oh shit.*

The storm building outside added to the strangeness of the moment. Ada Mae and Verna, in their polyester dresses and crisp white caps, stood beside Mervin and across the make shift bed from Jonas. Lester stepped back, but was closer to the action than Daniel and I. He smoothed his scraggly beard down his chest.

Jonas spoke in German, mumbling words that were unintelligible to me. I leaned forward, resting my chin on my hand.

He paused and looked at me, and the breath caught in my throat. His clear eyes glinted. A tremor passed through me, but I didn't look away. Jonas tilted his head, raising one eyebrow and turned back to Mervin.

I exhaled. I didn't bother to check Daniel's reaction, not wanting to miss anything that Jonas was doing.

His voice rose, becoming powerful enough to be heard over the advancing thunder booms and the heavy rain making a million sharp taps on the tin roof. When I glanced at Ada Mae and Verna, they had their eyes closed and were moving their mouths in what I assumed was a silent prayer. A quick glimpse at Lester proved he was doing the same.

I pulled myself from Jonas' ramblings to look at Daniel. He was watching the scene, eyes wide. I relaxed a little. At least he wasn't participating in whatever was going on.

Jonas put one of his hands on Mervin's forehead and rested the other on the boy's chest. His words, chanting to be more precise, gained volume. My heart raced with the building intensity of his voice. The air in the room took on a humid, thick consistency, almost as if a window had opened, allowing the rain to blow in. When I searched around, the windows were all shut. The wind howled outside. Branches scraped the glass and lightning lit up the room sporadically.

With wider eyes, I studied everyone's faces. The Amish still had their eyes closed, praying fervently. Daniel seemed to be holding his breath. Something was off in the room—hazy like, strange. My own mind was clouding over, heavy. I was tired. I fought the sensation, forcing myself to take a deep breath.

Mervin arched from the table, taking a gasping gulp of air. He dropped back onto the wood with a thud. His body was limp and memories from the time I'd spent in the abandoned barn with the Amish men rushed back to me.

I stood up, pulling my gun from the holster strapped at my waist. I aimed it at Jonas.

"Step away from him," I ordered.

5

DANIEL

I bolted upright and the blood drained from my head at dizzying speed. I wanted to touch Serenity's shoulder, but didn't dare, fearing that in her jumpy state, she might pull the trigger.

A faint smile touched Jonas' lips. He didn't raise his hands, but he did back away from Mervin. Ada Mae and the girl stood frozen. The girl's eyes were saucer sized. Ada Mae's flashed with humor, matching her twitching lips.

Another roll of thunder boomed and a blast of lightning immediately followed it. The candles illuminated the room in an eerie light. The west-facing windows revealed a break in the storm clouds and blue skies. In about five minutes, the sun would be shining again.

Serenity strode to Mervin's side, not taking her eyes from Jonas. She managed to point the gun at him while she felt for a pulse at Mervin's neck. She lowered the gun, slipping it back into the holster.

Her face flushed, but her voice was cool. "You have to understand, I couldn't take any chances with the boy's life."

A quivering look of confusion passed over Jonas' face when he met Serenity's hard gaze. No one else dared to move. Without turning his head, Jonas called out, "Mervin, wake up. It's time to walk on your new legs."

Serenity looked down at Mervin along with everyone else. The boy stirred, taking a deep breath. His eyes popped open. He rubbed them with his fingers and struggled to sit up, swaying as he straightened. Ada Mae slipped around the table. She grasped his arm to help him step down from the table. Lester hung back. He met my worried frown with a reassuring smile. My mother and father believed Jonas had the healing gift and so did Lester. Whether the man used his powers for evil purposes was anyone's guess, though.

Mervin leaned on Ada Mae as he slid off the table, his boots catching his weight with only a slight wobble. He paused to glance at Verna. She beamed at him. He returned the smile more shyly. I couldn't help grinning at the obvious puppy love.

Mervin took a sharp breath and then a step. Ada Mae stayed with him for several more steps before she let go. At first the boy's steps were tentative, searching for the pain that had plagued him for months. I thought back to the times I'd met him for lunch or walked along the river at his side. He'd been pretty messed up after his brother had killed Naomi, not sure if he wanted to remain Amish. I offered to help the kid, not just because he was my friend's son, but because I knew how he felt. I'd battled with the same questions and doubts, but with the pretty Amish girl watching his every step with rapt concern, I knew exactly where he'd end up.

Mervin's stride became surer and springier. After a little jump and a skip, he exclaimed, "The pain's gone—I'm healed!"

Serenity rolled her eyes and exhaled.

"*Denki, denki,*" Lester thanked Jonas, his face beaming. He reverted back to English. "I'll bring that bull calf over to you tomorrow."

"No need to hurry. Whenever you're heading back this way will be soon enough." Jonas' face hardened. "I expect you'll put those fresh legs to good use. Rebellion must not enter your heart, lest you tempt God. Our Lord took the pain away. He can bring it back."

I cringed inwardly at the religious reference, but said nothing. Serenity stood tight lipped.

"Ada, Verna, please escort the Lapps to their buggy. The Sheriff and Daniel have waited long enough to ask their questions," Jonas said.

"But you're exhausted," Ada Mae pointed out as she hesitated joining the others. Lester tipped his hat at me and made his escape. Mervin took the time to offer me a smile before he walked through the door beside Verna.

"I'll be fine," Jonas assured her. He nodded toward the door. She sighed loudly, but didn't argue.

When only Serenity, Jonas and I remained in the room, Jonas pointed to the chairs at the kitchen table. "I can make a pot of coffee if you'd like."

"That won't be necessary," Serenity said in a business-like manner as she took the chair closest to the wall. She had a view of the entire room and the doorway. I worked to keep the smile from my mouth. She was always the cop.

I sat in the chair beside her and Jonas settled across from us. For the first time I noticed his drooping eyes and pale face. Just as saving Lester had taking the life out of Ma, Jonas seemed to be thoroughly spent as well.

If Serenity saw the exhaustion on his face, she didn't acknowledge it.

"What ailment were you treating Fannie Kuhns for?" she asked.

His brows rose. "Fannie? It was her mother, Irene, I was treating. She suffers from gall bladder stones and asthma." He shrugged. "I provided her with a green tea infused with milk thistle. It's a common herbal remedy."

It made sense to me, and the easy manner in which Jonas spoke seemed to indicate truthfulness. I swiveled to look at Serenity.

"Are you saying that you never administered any teas or herbs to Fannie Kuhns?" Serenity asked.

I thought I glimpsed Jonas' eyes tear up and his Adam's apple rise as he swallowed, but when I blinked, his face was neutral, and his eyes dry. I chalked it up to my imagination.

"No. I wasn't under the impression that she had any medical problems," Jonas replied, returning her stare. "It's a shame that she died. If I'd been aware of her problem, I might have been able to help. At the very least, I would have advised her to see an English doctor for a thorough checkup."

"It's been brought to my attention that you're better than most midwives at delivering babies. Why wouldn't you treat the woman on your own?" Serenity plowed on.

He leaned back, taking a careful breath. "I didn't know of her condition. If she had come to me, I wouldn't have been able to help her."

"*Why?*" Serenity asked, drawing out the word with extra emphasis.

"She wasn't married. Her pregnancy was a sin," he said the words slowly, as if his statement was obvious. "An emergency situation is different, of course, but as long as she had other options for medical help, she would have had to seek them out."

My gaze followed Serenity's to the window. The sun pierced through the swiftly moving clouds. Faint rumbles from the storm as it moved away could still be heard.

Serenity's next words surprised me.

"Why treat Irene's gall bladder problems with herbs? Why not do what you just did with Mervin?" Her voice was light, but her stare was intense.

Jonas glanced at me. "She really doesn't understand our ways at all, does she?"

I shook my head, avoiding Serenity's gaze when she turned in my direction.

"It's God who decides who will be healed, not me—and not the patient," Jonas said, dropping his voice. "Confess your trespasses to one another, and pray for one another, that you may be healed. The effective, fervent prayer of a righteous man avails much. James five sixteen."

"You mean to say that God heals some, while abandoning others?" I found my voice.

Jonas' strange blue eyes settled on me. The look of disappointment on his face was evident. He must have thought some of my strict, religious upbringing would have stuck with me. In truth, it had, but whenever my people preached about sinning and sinners, I took it personally.

"It's the Lord's will who is saved and who isn't. Sometimes a man, woman or child must learn a lesson before they're gifted with a healing, then of course, they must cross paths with a *real* healer."

"How do you know when someone like Mervin or Irene are deserving of a healing?" Serenity asked.

"The Lord guides me to my patients in dreams and visions. I don't expect you to believe what I'm talking about. Outsiders rarely understand." Jonas stifled a yawn. "If you'll excuse me, I'm going to lie down. If you have any more questions, you can return another day."

"You aren't heading out of town any time soon, are you Mr. Peachey?" Serenity said, rising from her seat.

"Oh, no. I'll be here when you need me. Rest assured."

Silence hung in the air between me and Serenity while I pulled onto the road, heading back to town. I glanced sideways at her. She stared out the window. Her finger tapped against her thigh.

"What are you thinking?" I dared to ask. Serenity was un-characteristically reserved. I was beginning to worry about her state of mind.

She sighed. "Actually, I'm replaying that entire crazy scene over in my head, trying to figure out what the hell happened back there."

I cracked a smile. That was the Serenity I knew and loved.

"It's always an unnerving experience to witness a healing. There are forces…" I paused, searching for the right words. "…present that feel unnatural in a way."

"Exactly!" Serenity exclaimed. "I didn't see anything, but it felt as if something else was in the room with us. For the life of me, I can't decide whether it was good or bad." Serenity snorted. "No one is going to believe me."

"I believe you."

Serenity barked a laugh. "That's different. You're used to this kind of insanity. How many times have you witnessed a healing, by the way?"

I breathed deeply, thinking back to my childhood and counting the incidences. "Other than Ma healing Lester, there were three times. Two were by my great-grand *Mammi*. She's the one that passed the gift down to Ma. She laid her hands on an infant who came into the world as blue as the evening sky and completely still. I was only about six at the time myself, so I don't remember it very well, but I'll never forget the giant gulp of air the baby took and the oppressive heaviness that hung in the air when I'd snuck a peek through the crack in the door. The next time was at a livestock sale. I was probably about thirteen. Great-grand *Mammi* was ancient by then. She shuffled around with a cane and her hair was as white as snow. I was standing beside her, gazing into a pen at some bulls that were going to be driven into the stock shoot. A cowboy was climbing along the top of the corral, working his way to the far gate when one of the bigger bulls slammed its head into the panel. The cowboy lost his balance and fell into the pen. A huge bull gored the man with its long, curved horns. I knew that man was a goner.

"Several cowboys shimmied over the fence to help their friend. Luckily one of them had a cattle prod. He distracted the attacking bull long enough for the others to drag the injured man from the pen. His gut was bleeding and his pale face was pained. I remember *Mammi* asking him in English whether he believed the Lord was his savior. The man's eyes opened and he managed a limp nod. 'Yes ma'am, I do,' he'd answered weakly.

"*Mammi* laid her hands on the outsider just like she had the tiny, newborn infant. The air became heavy and the lights flickered. *Mammi* kept her hands on the man until the emergency personnel arrived. I distinctly remember the paramedic commenting that he was surprised that such a large wound wasn't bleeding more. The man recovered fully. I even saw him working the cattle at a sale the following year."

When I grew quiet, Serenity said coaxingly, "You said you'd witnessed three times, what was the third?"

Even though the storm had passed, the sky was dotted with swiftly moving clouds. Intermittently, a cloud passed over the sun, causing the sky to darken. The clouds blew by and the sun brightened the wet roadway once again.

I took a shaky breath. "I was fifteen. Our family traveled to Ohio to visit cousins. At least that's what I was told. Later I found out the truth. Ma had been diagnosed with breast cancer. Father sought out Jonas to do a healing on her. In a very creepy fashion, Jonas was expecting our arrival. He'd dreamed about it the week before. He agreed to a healing. My siblings and I were told stay in the guest room. Of course I didn't listen. I snuck out the window while my sister and brother begged me stay."

"What did you see?" Serenity asked, her voice breathy.

"Nothing. That's the really scary part. Just when I was rising up on my tip toes to peek through the window, I became dizzy. I must have fainted. The next thing I remember is my father splashing a cup of water on my face. When I opened my eyes, the first person I saw was Ma. She was peering over Father's shoulder at me, smiling. Her cancer was gone." I shook my head to dislodge the uncomfortable memory. "I can't explain it. She never had any radiation or chemotherapy. The English doctor was stunned. It was truly a miracle."

Silence drifted in the cab for a moment before Serenity found her voice. "Was it a miracle or someone selling their soul to the devil?" she asked with a frown.

I had to be honest. "I don't know."

6

SERENITY

"It's a good thing you're finally here, Serenity. Bobby is driving me crazy, checking in every five minutes, asking for you," Rosie grumbled.

She had been working in the Blood Rock's Sheriff's department for over thirty years. She still dyed her hair blonde and kept it swept up in a high bun. She was always smartly dressed and an even smarter thinker.

I smiled at her. The woman's combative relationship with Bobby amused me. "Call him and tell him we're on our way."

"I wouldn't walk too fast. Won't hurt him to hold his horses for a change," she called out as Daniel and I reached the stairs down to the morgue. I didn't turn around to respond.

"Were Rosie and Bobby ever romantically involved?" Daniel asked.

"Funny you should ask. Todd told me they were indeed an item back in the day. I guess Rosie was a little too high strung for him. When she was hired on as the receptionist in the department, it nearly drove Bobby mad." I glanced at Daniel, who was grinning. "He's learned to deal with the situation over the years, but it isn't easy for him."

I knocked on the door leading into the morgue. Bobby called out with a gruff voice to enter, and I pressed down on the handle. I wrinkled my nose at the onslaught of cleaning products and formaldehyde that assaulted my senses. Without much thought, I went into barely-breathing mode. It was the only way I could handle the autopsy room.

Daniel swallowed and his face tightened. I forced my attention to Fannie Kuhns' naked body lying on the examination table. Several overhead lights shone down on her gray skin. Her eyes were closed. She was on the plump side, with round and full breasts. My eyes were drawn to her long brown hair piled up around her head.

It was never easy looking at a dead person who only hours before had been one of the living, but I'd become desensitized to it. I'd seen a fair amount of death lately.

Bobby had his back turned to us, scribbling notes. I went to the counter and plucked two pairs of latex gloves from the box. I handed a pair to Daniel and squeezed my fingers into the other one.

"What do you have for me, Bobby?"

Bobby cleared his throat and picked up his clipboard. He turned and peered over his glasses at us.

"I have some more tests before I write the official report, but on the Q.T., I'm fairly certain the cause of death is a massive obstetric hemorrhage. Basically, she bled to death."

"Have you determined the cause of the bleeding?" I glanced at Fannie's face. A shiver passed through me. She was only in her twenties.

SECRETS IN THE GRAVE

Bobby sighed, following my gaze. "Catastrophic bleeding episodes rarely happen in the middle of pregnancy, but spontaneous hemorrhage isn't unheard of, either. Sometimes no cause can even be determined."

"Don't say that, Bobby. I'm trusting you to figure out what happened to Fannie." I narrowed my eyes.

He ignored my look and statement. "What I can tell you for sure is she lost about three and a half pints of blood. When I inspected the room where she died, I didn't find the evidence of that much blood, which leads me to believe the mother and sister took the time to dispose of the bloody linens before we arrived."

"That's not so uncommon with Amish women. They're often present for births, deaths and the treatment of sick individuals. I wouldn't be surprised if they removed the soiled bedding. They're extremely thoughtful about cleanliness," Daniel pointed out.

"My issue isn't so much with the cleaning up of the evidence, so to speak, but that it would have taken the woman a while to bleed out that much." Bobby shifted his gaze to me. "Why wouldn't they have called the paramedics or even their own Amish healer before she died?"

"That's a good question and one I don't have the answer to—yet," I said. "Perhaps the family didn't know she was bleeding. She probably went into shock before she even lost enough blood to kill her."

Bobby nodded. "That is true." He removed his glasses and rubbed his eyes. "How did the visit with the medicine man go?"

I turned to Daniel. He shrugged and leaned against the counter. It felt wrong to talk over a person's dead body, but I shook off the dirty feeling and replied, "I witnessed a miraculous healing."

Bobby leaned in over Fannie, ignoring her all together. His eyes were bright.

"It was the weirdest thing I've ever seen," I admitted. "Do you remember Mervin Lapp, the little brother of Naomi's killer?" Bobby nodded. "The injury he sustained when his brother hit him in the leg with the butt end of his shotgun never really healed. He was limping around in pain, and the medical professionals told him he'd need future surgeries to fully recover." I ran my hand through my hair. Talking about it made me feel like a crazy person. "Well, Jonas healed him—right before my very eyes."

"I've heard of such healings." Bobby grunted. "I wish I'd been there to witness it. I've always wondered if a person has that kind of power, why don't they heal everyone?"

"I basically asked the same question. Jonas is a conduit for God's healing power. And God decides who gets healed," I said.

"Fascinating. I'd like to hear more about it over lunch tomorrow." Bobby set down his clipboard. He pulled the plastic sheet over Fannie. "I don't have time for it now. I want to get the samples sent off to the state lab this evening. Whatever Fannie was drinking in that cup might hold some of the answers we're looking for."

"Sounds like a plan." A headache began to throb on the side of my forehead. The strange afternoon had caught up with me.

Daniel and I left Bobby at his desk, sorting out the samples and placing them in urgent delivery boxes. We dragged back up the steps, lost in thought. Part of me was revisiting the healing I'd witnessed and the other was thinking about Fannie and her tragic death.

I also wondered whether Daniel would spend the night. He'd been staying over at my apartment more frequently lately, and I'd noticed that he'd left his toothbrush beside mine that morning. The rapid developments in the relationship left me feeling rushed. It was odd that Daniel wanted to spend so much time at my place. He lived in a beautiful log cabin on the outskirts of town. It was much nicer than the one bedroom efficiency I was renting while I waited for the insurance company to conclude their investigation into the arson of my last home.

There was still the dreaded conversation that Daniel had started that morning to worry about. Would he bring up the matter again? Clenching my teeth, I glanced over at him, only to find him smirking back at me as if he'd read my mind.

"It's almost quitting time," he said, pointing to his watch.

I stopped and tilted my head. "I was thinking that maybe we could drive out to your parents' house and ask them some questions." I felt cowardly about my ulterior motives, but shrugged it off.

"Tonight?" Daniel scowled. "I don't think that's a good idea. More than likely, Aaron has called a meeting with the ministers that will include Father. And Ma is probably still at the Kuhns' house. She's close with Irene. She'll want to be there to comfort her and help make arrangements."

Everything he said made perfect sense, but I still felt the prickle of irritation that he'd so easily shot down my attempt to avoid being alone with him that evening. He'd definitely take advantage of the situation. I'd be forced to discuss something that I didn't want to and that was something I wasn't ready for.

"I'm afraid I have a lot of paperwork to sift through tonight. It's probably best if you head on home. We can catch up tomorrow morning, maybe even head back out to the Amish settlement to talk to your parents and a few other people," I said, hoping he wouldn't argue.

"You have to eat. Why don't we at least have dinner at Nancy's Diner first? You can come back here to finish whatever work you need to," Daniel offered. His eyes were not only wide with expectancy, but also daring me to refuse.

I was about to come up with an excuse when Rosie called out. "Serenity, don't you dare leave yet. The new assistant DA stopped by to meet you. She's waiting in your office."

My brows rose and I groaned. Elayne Weaver wasn't supposed to start the job for a few weeks. I wasn't even aware that she'd made the move.

"Sorry, I'm going to have to talk to her." I feigned disappointment.

"I'll hang out until you're finished. How long can it take to say hello and welcome her to the neighborhood?"

"Whatever," I muttered, turning on my heels. I felt Daniel's presence behind me when I reached my office and opened up the door.

The woman looking out the window was not at all what I was expecting. Her black heels were at least four inches high, making her already tall, slender frame resemble a model. Even though she wasn't officially on the job, she wore a tailored black skirt and cream colored blouse that had a feminine ruffle at the neckline. Her hair was exceptionally long, thick and sleekly black. She wore minimal makeup on a flawless, oval face. In a single glimpse, I was jealous of her.

She left the window with an outstretched hand. "Sheriff Adams, it's such a pleasure to finally meet you. I'm Elayne Weaver. Mayor Ed Johnson had the nicest things to say about you. I even was introduced to your deputy, Todd Roftin. He's quite the character."

Elayne's voice was as feminine as her clothing, her figure and her face. She was cheerleader material all the way. Back in high school, I hated girls like her. I was a jeans and sneakers, soccer playing sort of a girl. I only wore heels to weddings and funerals.

I recovered quickly from her friendly bombardment. "It's nice to meet you, Elayne. I hope you'll enjoy living here in Blood Rock. It's a little rural for some people's tastes," I said with forced perkiness.

"Oh, I'm quite familiar with Blood Rock," she said.

I tilted my head, "Really?"

"This used to be my home."

"Elayne, is that really you?" Daniel asked, stepping through the doorway.

"Why, if it isn't Daniel Bachman! I never thought I'd see you again. Figured you would have moved on from this town ages ago," she exclaimed, tucking her hair behind her ear in a quick motion.

My head snapped in Daniel's direction. He wasn't looking at me at all. He was staring at Elayne.

"How do you two know each other?" I asked, fearing the answer.

"We grew up together. Elayne used to be Amish," Daniel said in an awestruck manner.

I took a deep breath and swallowed. *Now my day is complete.*

7

"**H**e just ditched me," I grumbled, taking a bite of the bacon cheeseburger.

"Now that's not exactly what you said a moment ago," Todd said. "You told the man to go on and eat without you—that you had work to do."

I glanced at Bobby. In one hand he held a French fry and in the other, a medical journal magazine. He seemed to be ignoring the conversation completely, but I wasn't fooled. Every so often, he'd look up and make a comment.

"What do you think, Bobby?" I leaned over the table. "Was it right for Daniel to go out to dinner with *that* woman?" I took another ripping bite of my sandwich. "I think that kind of behavior warrants being mad at him."

Bobby laid the magazine down and met my demanding gaze. "From what you already told us, Daniel asked you out to dinner first—and you didn't answer—then the new DA showed up and he invited her to join the two of you for dinner. It was an understandable offer since Elayne Weaver was there to introduce herself to you in the first place. When you declined Daniel's offer, you not only hurt his pride, you also opened the situation up for him to be alone with his long-lost Amish girlfriend."

I lowered my voice as I replied, "Ms. Weaver wasn't his girlfriend. She's actually a couple of years older than him. It was her little brother that Daniel was friends with."

Nancy's Diner was packed for the lunchtime rush. I wasn't exactly worried about someone overhearing our conversation, but you could never be too careful when gossiping.

"Since they grew up in the same community and both left, I'd say they have a lot in common. She isn't hard on the eyes, either," Todd said, smirking with a faraway look on his face as if remembering the woman in detail.

I smacked Todd's shoulder. "How can you talk that way when Heather is seven months pregnant with your baby? You men are all the same. A pretty new woman shows up and you turn to braindead, cheating mush."

"That's not true. I would never cheat on Heather. There's nothing wrong with noticing an attractive woman. That happens all the time. Actually hooking up is another story altogether." Todd had a sort of pleading, please-believe-me look on his face. "Even though the new DA is a beautiful woman, I can tell she doesn't have the sick sense of humor my Heather does or the easy-going, laid-back manner, either. I would never risk losing Heather for someone as high maintenance and serious as that woman is. I bet neither would Daniel."

"I don't know about that. You should have seen him staring awestruck at her, like she was an angel or something. Then she began asking him about these different Amish people and who they'd married and how many kids they had. I felt completely out of my element," I admitted.

"So! You should have stayed with your man. Now that woman has her claws sunk straight into him, especially since you aren't very nice to him," Todd said.

"How have I *not* been nice to Daniel?" I demanded, glancing around. Everyone in the neighboring booths were turned our way, trying to listen. I stared hard back at them until their eyes dropped to their food.

Todd raised his finger and was about to list all the ways when Bobby interrupted, shutting him up.

"Now hold on, Todd. I've spent some time observing Serenity and Daniel's interactions with each other. I have no doubt that Daniel is in love with Serenity, but Serenity isn't sure about her feelings. She needs more time to work them out. She's not the type of person to be forced into feeling something she isn't sure about. I think her aloof behavior is acceptable under the circumstances."

Aloof behavior? I didn't think that I'd been aloof with Daniel. Most nights we ate dinner together, followed by passionate sex. Bobby nailed my feelings, though. I was torn about Daniel. A part of me wanted to surrender to him and the rest wanted to run away. I didn't even like the idea of being in love. It scared the hell out of me.

Todd raised his brows. "Besides the Amish heritage thing, Daniel seems like a good guy. He tries hard to please you. What's the deal anyway?"

I leaned back on the red plastic seat and sighed. "I'm not going to get into my personal relationship hang ups. We don't have a long enough lunch break."

"I'm always available as your sounding board," Todd offered.

I wasn't exactly sure how to respond. Luckily, Bobby saved me. "Why don't you tell me more about the ritualistic healing you witnessed? You said it was weird. How so?"

I looked out the diner's window at the overcast day beyond. Main Street was busy, a constant stream of passing cars. There were a fair number of men in suits and women in skirts and heels walking along the tree lined sidewalk. The town of Blood Rock was growing—just like the Amish settlement on the edge of my jurisdiction. Sometimes it was hard to believe that only fifteen miles way lived a large number of people trapped in a time warp from the nineteenth century.

I returned my gaze to Bobby. "Jonas Peachey was praying in German, mumbling really. It began to storm. He dipped his hands in a type of anointing oil and laid one hand on the boy's forehead, and the other on his chest. The atmosphere in the room was thick for a moment, then Mervin gulped for air. I thought he was dying and pulled my gun on the medicine man." Bobby's eyes widened, but he didn't interrupt me. I heard Todd's intake of breath at my side. "When I checked Mervin, his pulse was fine and he was breathing. A few minutes later, he was up bouncing around the room on what appeared to be new legs."

"Hmm." Bobby frowned.

"How can the air be thick in a room?" Todd remarked.

I thought, searching for the right words to describe the scene at the Amish house. "It was oppressive, almost as if something or someone else was there with us."

Todd whistled the Twilight Zone theme song. I rolled my eyes.

"Were there candles or incense burning?" Bobby inquired.

"Yeah, candles were lit around the room."

"I've heard that certain aromas can alter the mind's perception and even induce mild hallucinations. The candles might be your answer," Bobby mused.

I was pondering what he said when my radio and Todd's went off. I motioned for Todd to respond to his outside of the booth as I hit the button on mine. As Kristen, one of the local dispatch officers spoke, my mouth dropped and I stood to peer out the window better. A second later, Todd looked over my shoulder.

Across the road was the Blood Rock Savings Bank. The front doors of the three story brick building were closed. There was some foot traffic going past the bank, but no one was coming out of it.

"Todd and I are both at Nancy's. We're going to investigate. Bring in all available officers. Block off east and west Main Street, Sycamore Boulevard and Racing Road. Oh, and contact Sheriff Gilroy in Alma and notify him of the situation. If they somehow get past us, they'll surely be heading toward the interstate and into his county."

Sirens blared, becoming louder by the second when I broke off contact with Kristen. "You stay here," I told Bobby as I slid from the booth.

Spotting Nancy, the owner of the diner, behind the counter, I waved her over. "We have a situation at the bank. Don't let anyone leave the diner." I looked over my shoulder, back at Bobby. "Help Nancy with an announcement," I instructed him. He nodded with a tight expression.

"Sure thing, kiddo. We'll take care of business here," Nancy said. I was turning away when her hand snaked out and she grasped my arm. "Be careful."

"Always am."

Todd and I had our side arms out when we reached the cruiser. Todd wasted no time unlocking the door and reaching for his riot shotgun. He swapped weapons. I preferred my 9 MM, especially in tight places.

"Can you believe this? These yahoos are damn ballsy to attempt an armed robbery at the bank," Todd breathed.

Jeremy was the first to park along the curb. Three more cruisers took positions behind him, across from the bank.

Before Jeremy was out of the vehicle, I called out, "Clear the street of pedestrians. I want to see only uniforms on this block."

Jeremy went into action. I paused long enough to direct the other officers to take positions around the bank.

"Or damn stupid," I finally replied, glancing at Todd. With his military buzzed haircut, bulging biceps and aviator sunglasses, he looked every bit the Hollywood cop. "Everyone in this town knows that most of Blood Rock's law enforcement eats a couple of meals a day at the diner." I waved for him to follow me down the narrow alley along the east side of the building. The rock wall that paralleled the bank was covered with ivy and shaded by several enormous oak trees. There weren't many windows on that side of the building, and if memory served me correctly, the bank's offices were located on this side, too.

"Are we going in?" Todd asked. The pitch of his voice was high. He was juiced up on adrenaline.

"Sure are. There's a door back here that leads out to the garbage bin. We'll see if we can sneak in without being noticed. We need to know how many men there are."

"Good plan, boss," Todd said with the kind of steady determination I appreciated in times like these.

We stopped at the metal door, pressing our backs up against the brick wall. Todd was closer to the door. He looked sideways at me and I nodded. With fluid movement, he turned the handle, opening the door. I sprang around him, pointing my gun down the long, empty corridor.

I motioned for Todd to follow and he let the door close behind us, blotting out the daylight and leaving only the dim illumination from the lightbulbs dangling from the ceiling. The building was historic and not built to repel armed robberies. Hell, the place smelled like mothballs. Perhaps that's why this particular bank was picked in the first place.

We silently bypassed several closed doors, making our way closer to the front of the building where the tellers, bank vault and lobby were. I paused beside a larger door and pressed my head to the wood. I heard muffled voices. Meeting Todd's gaze, I made a quick decision.

This time, I opened the door. Todd went in first, his shotgun poised in front of him, and I followed on his heels. The room was small, crammed with three wooden desks and several metal file cabinets. Four middle-aged women huddled in the corner. One of them clutched her chest when we came through the door.

I instantly recognized Mabel Cunningham, the county clerk. She rushed forward.

"Thank the Lord, you're here," Mabel whispered. Her pudgy face smiled.

"Whoa, we're not out of the woods. How many are there?" I said.

"Four. And they're all wearing black ski masks," Mabel said.

"Original thinkers," Todd commented.

"Are they all armed?" I asked Mabel.

"Sure are." She glanced back at the other women. "I think they were carrying rifles, weren't they?" Two of the women nodded, and the other began crying. "If you go through that door—" Mabel pointed to one of the three doors in the room. "—and take a short hallway, you'll come to glass doors that lead out into the lobby. The vault and tellers are on the other side. You might be able to safely get a peek for yourselves. I had just stepped into the hallway when it began. They got everyone down on the floor."

"How many patrons?"

Mabel didn't hesitate, shrugging. "I'd say fourteen, maybe fifteen all together. Thursday afternoons are one of the bank's busiest times of the week."

I nodded at Mabel's calm, clear and concise information. "You ladies take the backdoor. Keep your hands up. I have officers positioned out there. Tell them what you told me and remind them to wait to enter the building until I give the all clear or they hear gunshots."

Mabel nodded. She ushered the other woman out the door, only turning back to whisper, "Praying for you, Sheriff."

I hit the switch on my radio. "Turn off your radio," I ordered. "We don't want them going off at the wrong time."

Todd turned his off and followed me into the hallway. We stepped lightly over the long, Oriental rug covering the floor. The door with the glass windows was directly ahead of us.

Todd raised his gun, but I stopped him. "Look first, attack later."

"I'll follow your lead."

I had my gun up in front of me as I walked sideways down the hallway, my back against the wall. With each step, the voices grew louder. I separated the voices the best I could, trying to determine how spread out they were. Before I reached the glass panels, I suspected that two men were close together on one side of the lobby and the other two were spread out on the other side. I didn't hear anyone else and that made my stomach clench.

Todd pressed up against the wall and I ducked down, crawling over to the door. With my heart pounding, I rose up on my knees, peeking through the frosted edge of the lowest panel of glass. Inching higher, I had a view of most of the lobby.

As I thought, one man was standing at the entrance doors and another was off to the side. Both men were average build and height, and they had their guns pointed at the men and woman lying on the floor. I glimpsed the prone form of a small girl beside her gray-haired grandmother.

I couldn't see the other two, but I could hear them. They were yelling at the tellers, demanding that they open the vault. When the voice levels rose, Todd began fidgeting. I held up my hand. Our eyes met. He took a purposeful breath, calming himself.

One of the robbers jumped from the counter, coming into view. He took the butt end of his semiautomatic gun, and using it like a baseball bat, struck the legs of one of the men on the ground. The gray haired man shrieked, curling up into the fetal position. My eyes widened. The mayor. Then I noticed the long, silky dark hair next to him. It was none other than the new assistant DA, Elayne Weaver.

At almost the same time the mayor was assaulted, a man on the other side of him rose, showing his face. He was holding a small handgun.

When I saw Daniel, I muttered, "Dammit."

I looked at Todd. "We just ran out of time."

8

DANIEL

"**D**aniel remodeled our house last year, did an amazing job. I'm sure this loft of his will be first rate," Mayor Ed said over his shoulder to Elayne. I looked away, my face heating. I didn't mind the praise, but the mayor was putting it on a little too thick. Elayne grinned at me, sensing my discomfort. Maybe it was an Amish thing. We were raised not to enjoy being the center of attention.

"I have no doubt that it will be perfect for my needs," Elayne said.

"It's nothing fancy. Just the top floor of the Murphey building. When I bought the property last year, it was my intention to stay as true to its historical heritage as I could. I've only had time to finish the top unit." I shrugged.

The line for the teller moved up a person and I followed Elayne and the mayor another step forward.

"Don't be so damn modest, Daniel. You've done a wonderful job restoring that old building." He turned to Elayne. "City council was seriously considering tearing it down. Kids were sneaking in to party and God-knows-what late at night.

It wasn't safe anymore. Daniel gave us a better option. The townspeople are thrilled, making me a happy mayor."

Elayne leaned in. "I really do appreciate you taking the time from your busy day to show me the apartment."

"It's no problem. I had some errands to run in town anyway. The bank was the perfect place to meet up. After I make my deposit, I'll take you there. When you're finished looking, I'll drop you back off at the mayor's office," I said with a guarded smile.

Elayne smiled back, her brown eyes twinkling. She was still very much the same girl I'd once known. She'd always been flirty, but unlike the other girls, she had a curious mind. It didn't surprise me that she left the Amish to pursue an education and career.

I remembered when she got into trouble for sneaking in a pile of romance novels given to her by one of the English drivers. It had been quite the scandal. She'd sat on the splintery bench in front of the entire congregation while Aaron recited her sins. She'd been shunned for two weeks. Not a terrible punishment by Amish standards, but enough to help push her out the door.

I couldn't help noticing that Elayne was the polar opposite of Serenity. While Elayne was a tall brunette with dark eyes, my girlfriend was blonde, blue eyed and several inches shorter. Elayne was overly warm and friendly, compared to Serenity's cool aloofness. Although Elayne was an intelligent woman and had grown up on a farm, she didn't have a lot of common sense. Serenity overflowed with the ability to make decisions under fire. Elayne was more about showing off and Serenity was all about the cause. Even though they were both career women, Elayne had explained to me last night that she had a specific timeline to be married and have two children within four years. Serenity didn't even want to broach the subject of a family.

Strangely, the very things I wanted from Serenity, Elayne was searching for. She understood my upbringing and had struggled with her own shunning the same way I had. She wanted commitment and kids. We had a lot in common, but for all that, it didn't make the dark-haired beauty appealing.

After having been with a woman like Serenity, a person with so many layers I hadn't even scratched the surface of, Elayne seemed boring. She wasn't the challenge Serenity was. Being around Elayne had only hammered in how much I loved Serenity. I'd probably give up having a family to be with her. I certainly couldn't imagine ever walking away, but in the end, I may not have a choice in the matter. Serenity's fear of commitment could ruin everything.

My mood soured at the thought. I forced a smile at Elayne as we took another step up in line. The day was ticking by slowly. I wanted to get the apartment showing over with so I could head to the sheriff's office to talk to Serenity.

I glanced out the window at the overcast day, wondering if Serenity was eating a late lunch with Todd and Bobby across the street at the diner. They had a lot to talk about with the circumstances of Fannie Kuhns' death and the strange healing that Mervin received from Jonas. With a surge of hopefulness, I thought that if I hurried Elayne through the loft, I might even get to the diner before she left.

"Get down! Get down!" voices shouted from behind.

I whirled to see four men slipping through the entrance. They each wore a black ski mask and carried rifles raised above their heads. The weight of my .38 Special was heavy against my leg and I sent a prayer of thanks up that I'd taken the carry and conceal class upon returning from Poplar Springs.

I deliberated quickly. I was outnumbered four to one. There was a real chance that these men might get the money and run, leaving everyone unharmed. I dropped to the ground with everyone else. My gaze slid over to Ed, who was attempting to use his cell phone.

"Don't be a fucking idiot!" the taller assailant cried, kicking the phone out of Ed's hands. Elayne scurried closer to me and I shot her a reassuring smile.

"Do you know who I am—" Ed began.

"I don't care if you're the damn mayor! Shut up and put your head down or I'll put a bullet in it."

The robber's words silenced everyone. Ginger Crawly and her granddaughter were not too far away. The little girl's face was wet with tears. Ginger's arm covered the girl, squeezing her tightly enough to quiet the child. My gaze met Ginger's. Her mouth twitched and she swallowed.

One of the men jumped onto the counter. Another went behind it, forcing the tellers against the wall. The man who had kicked Ed stood close by and the last one guarded the front doors.

"Here's how it's going to be," the man on the counter drawled with a southern accent. The one who had kicked Ed's phone sounded more northern, maybe even from Boston, making me think that these boys were all from out of town. "You're all going to lay on the floor until we get the money we want. If you behave, you'll live to post about this on social media tonight. If you give us any trouble, you'll be shot. How does that sound?" When no one answered, he repeated, "How does that sound, folks?"

This time people murmured agreement and nodded their heads.

"You, clean out their pockets" —the southerner motioned to the northerner with his gun— "while Batman gets into the vault."

As my face pressed against the cool tiles of the floor, the man behind the counter argued with the bank's manager about the protocol to get the vault open. The northerner made his way through the crowd on the floor, demanding that everyone empty their pockets. He used his foot to push the money into a pile. One older gentleman was forced to remove his watch and the women were ordered to throw their jewelry into the pile. I cringed as wedding rings clinked across the floor.

I couldn't help wondering how long it would take Serenity to show up. Surely one of the tellers had pushed a silent alarm beneath a desk by now. I took a deep breath, trying to slow my racing heart. It was just a matter of time before the robbers got what they wanted and left or Serenity and her department arrived.

When the northerner reached me, I threw out my billfold, with the envelope containing four thousand dollars inside it. The money was from a porch job I'd completed, and the deposit was supposed to pay the crew's weekly wages. Throwing the money away wasn't a complete disaster for the business, but it would make things uncomfortable for a couple of weeks.

My eyes wandered back to Ginger. She was on a fixed income. Whatever money she had in her purse was needed to put food on the table. The cold, hard tiles that were so uncomfortable on my body must be agonizing for the elderly woman. I'd built bookshelves in her living room some years earlier and I still remembered the delicious hot roast beef sandwich and homemade iced tea she'd served for lunch that day. Anger flared inside of me, constricting my chest.

"Nice," the northerner said. A small smile twitched on his mouth.

I looked away, fearing the man would see my hatred if our gazes locked.

The northerner paused at Elayne. "Aren't you a pretty piece of ass?"

He ran the toe of his boot along Elayne's leg until he reached her skirt. Elayne's eyes went wide and teary when the man lifted the material. I reached for the holster strapped to my leg, ready to grab my gun. I was betting I could shoot the man and get off one more shot before I was fired upon in return.

Indecision stalled my movement. If I fired, would the robbers shoot the other patrons? There was always a chance that innocent people would get shot when bullets began flying around. My gaze settled on Ginger's granddaughter. The girl sniffed, holding in her tears, staying my hand.

The two robbers behind the counter were still arguing with the manager about the vault and his ability to access it. As their voices rose higher, the northerner dropped his foot away from Elayne.

Elayne swallowed. I caught a glimpse of movement in the glass window to the side of the tellers' counter. It was so brief I thought I might have imagined it.

The raised voices turned to shouting. One of the robbers grabbed the bank manager, yanking him closer, and pressed the gun against his temple.

"I'll blow your fucking brains out if you don't open that God damn vault!"

"I'm sorry...it takes two of us to make the sequence...it's a security system," the small, bald man stuttered.

Surprising me even more than the fact that the bank was being robbed in the first place, Mayor Ed raised his head. In a quivering voice, he said, "There's no need for this to get ugly. Take our money and whatever is in the registers. Then be on your way. No one has to get hurt."

The other man jumped over the counter and whacked Ed's legs with the butt of his gun. He swung it around and aimed the barrel at Ed's face. The mayor screamed, "Stop!"

Hoping that my mind hadn't been playing tricks on me when I'd seen movement in the window, I grabbed my gun.

I didn't have time to say a prayer. I held the gun up and fired.

9

SERENITY

I aimed and shot through the glass. As shattered shards rained down, Todd took a shot through the now open panel. I shoved open the door. The man I'd aimed for was down. Todd's target was writhing near the doorway and Daniel's guy was in a heap a few feet from him.

Todd and I rounded the corner. Everyone behind the counter ducked. "Dammit," I growled. The fourth robber had a gun pressed to Barry's head. The bank manager's face had drained of all color, his eyes round.

"Give me what I want and I'll let him live," the man called out.

The sounds of muffled crying and the surviving robber's moans broke the silence. The silhouettes of uniformed officers beyond the front windows flashed. I switched my radio on and hit the button. "Stand down. We have a hostage situation."

My eyes skimmed over Daniel. He'd moved sideways to shield Elayne from harm. He had his gun raised, waiting for me to give him a signal. I averted my gaze and looked at Todd instead.

He tilted his head towards the end of the counter, raising his brows. I understood what he meant to do. Todd had done some sniper work when he'd served in the armed forces. He was better a shot than me.

I nodded and began talking. "What are your terms?"

"I have a car and driver waiting on the west side. You clear me a path to that car," the man answered.

Todd inched closer to the counter. I had to keep the robber talking.

"That sounds reasonable. Anything else?" I asked.

There was a silent pause. Todd glanced back at me, but kept moving.

"I didn't go to all this trouble for a handful of cash. You get this dimwit to open the fucking the vault."

I thought quickly. "Barry couldn't accommodate you without a second person's coding. Since I'm the Sheriff, I have both codes," I lied. "Here's how it's going to work. I'm going to take Barry's place. I'll open the vault and give you what you want."

I walked to the counter, ignoring Daniel's frown as he stood. The robber's gun was still pushed into the side of Barry's head. I couldn't see his face behind the mask, but his eyes were blue and troubled.

"I'm not stupid. The minute I let go of this loser, you're going to shoot me."

I swallowed against the pounding of my heart and focused. Lowering my gun for the man to see, I ejected the clip and set it on the counter. I was close enough to see four young women huddled together on the floor behind the counter only a few feet away from Barry and his assailant.

"Trust me now?" I asked.

"That asshole over there had better drop his gun." The robber jutted his chin at Daniel. His hands were too busy with his own gun and holding Barry to motion any other way.

"You heard the man. Drop it," I called out, but I didn't look Daniel's way.

An instant later, I heard the *thunk* of metal hitting the tiles.

"Better?" I asked nicely.

"Radio your people out there. Tell them I'm coming through the door with you on the end of this gun. If they try anything funny, I'll blow your brains out. Then they won't have a pretty sheriff anymore." The man tapped his foot fast and hard.

I raised the radio to my lips. "I'm trading places with the hostage. Continue to stand down. We're coming out the door."

A few more steps took me to the wooden-paneled, swinging door that led behind the counter. I reached over and flipped the latch, never taking my eyes from the target. My brows rose questioningly and he curtly nodded in return.

Once I was within reach, the robber shoved Barry toward the women. In a blink, the gun was inches from my head. The man's other hand grabbed my pony tail, jerking my head back. The sharp pain caused purple dots to pepper my vision.

The gunshot blasted loud in my ear, silencing the world.

I turned and drove my elbow into the man's neck, knocking him backwards, but the action wasn't needed. Todd's bullet had hit its mark. The man's brains covered the white wall behind him, but pulling my hair was something I had no tolerance for.

As my hearing returned, Todd radioed the officers outside to come into the building. A moment later, a sea of blue uniforms mingled with the patrons as they rose from the floor. Since it was a relatively small town, almost everyone knew everyone else. There was a cacophony of hushed conversations all around.

"Thank you so much, Sheriff," one of the tellers gushed as she stepped away from the dead man.

I forced a smile and motioned for her to join Jeremy at the end of the counter with the other tellers. I sighed, looking around. This was going to be a paperwork nightmare.

"That was splendid teamwork!" Mayor Ed exclaimed. He limped around the body to pat me on the back. "I have to admit, I was getting a little worried there." He barked an adrenaline filled laugh. Turning his head, he said, "Remarkable shot, Todd. I didn't know you had it in you."

Todd shook his head. If Ed had bothered reading anything about the deputies in his county, he'd have known that Todd was more than capable of putting a bullet between a man's eyes.

"Is it your intention to make sure I never leave the office?" Bobby joked, joining our group. Seeing his grin slowed my beating heart.

I chuckled. "Yep. This should keep you busy for a while." I glanced over at Todd. "I want to know who these idiots are and why they targeted the Blood Rock Bank, but let's get everyone out of here first."

"On it, boss," Todd said. He ushered the tellers from behind the counter to join the rest of the citizens filing out of the bank. Barry had somehow managed to get to the front of the line. It bugged me that he hadn't even paused to say thanks for saving his life. It wasn't surprising, though. On a good day, the man was a paralyzed pigeon.

"You were hit pretty hard, Ed. Why don't you get into one of those ambulances waiting at the curb? We'll take care of everything here," I suggested.

"I hope there's no permanent damage." Ed clutched his leg and limped away. "I'll meet with you and Bobby later today."

I looked across the room. Daniel stood beside the cushioned seats with Elayne, only a few inches between them. My eyes narrowed as I watched them. Elayne swished her hair over her shoulders while she quietly conversed with Daniel. He glanced up and met my stare. When he saw me, his brows arched. He said a few words to Ed and Elayne frowned, looking my way. Ed and Elayne walked out the door together and Daniel marched toward me.

I began sweating and the breath caught in my throat. My nerves had begun settling and I resented Daniel's effect on my body. I had too much going on to deal with conflicting emotions. Part of me wanted to shoot him for being nice to Elayne and the other wanted desperately to melt into him.

"Are you all right?" Daniel said when he reached me. He didn't try to embrace me, but then again, I didn't run into his arms, either.

My muscles tensed. "It's just part of the job."

Daniel licked his lips, glanced away, and then met my gaze again. "We need to talk. I don't like this wall that's developing between us."

"If you haven't noticed, I'm kind of busy here." I regretted my sarcasm when Daniel's eyes widened with hurt.

"I get that, but at some point you have to go home. Text me and I'll meet you there. Don't worry about the time. I'm not going to sleep until I hear from you."

We were finally going to have the conversation that I'd been avoiding for days. An unwanted tingle of relief washed over me, but my jealous nature wouldn't allow me to say okay. "Are sure you don't have dinner plans with Elayne?"

Daniel's face flushed. "No, I don't," he said and narrowed his eyes.

We were at an impasse when Bobby interrupted us.

"I just got a call from my friend at the state lab in Indianapolis about that tea cup," Bobby said.

Daniel's face went neutral and I sobered. I had all but forgotten about Fannie Kuhns with all the excitement in here.

"I'm almost afraid to ask what he had to say," I said.

Bobby nodded with tight lips. "There are still more tests to run, but two components of the tea have been identified." He paused to make sure that both Daniel and I were fully paying attention. "We were right about the peppermint. It was definitely in there. The other ingredient was not expected. Tansy ragwort."

I glanced at Daniel and he shrugged. "I don't know anything about poisonous plants, Bobby. Please elaborate—and quickly."

He didn't get the reaction he'd anticipated from either of us. Rolling his eyes, he said, "It's not a poison per se when handled properly. Before modern medicines, it was used to treat worms, fever, and repel insects. The colonists preserved meat with it and sometimes placed it on bodies before burial. Primitive cultures still use it today for similar purposes."

"Why would Fannie be drinking something like that?" I asked, holding up my finger to Jeremy, stalling him for a moment more. Behind Jeremy, there were two men in crisp, expensive suits waiting. I already guessed they were feds. They must have been in the area to arrive so quickly.

"There is another documented use for tansy that is similar to the parsley. It's an abortifacient."

"Is that what I think it is?"

"It can cause miscarriage when administered in high doses. It's impossible to tell the potency of the yellow flowering top of the plant by just looking at it. Where one flower may be completely benign, another can be toxic. Most herbalists shy away from the plant because of its unpredictable nature."

I dropped my voice. "Fannie might have been trying to induce her own abortion—or she could have been murdered?"

Bobby nodded solemnly.

An image of the young woman's naked body on the examination table flashed before my eyes. I shivered. It was hard to believe an Amish woman would choose to have an abortion, but I couldn't rule out the possibility, especially since she wasn't married. I never would have expected Esther Lapp to go to such illegal lengths to protect her son after he'd intentionally murdered Naomi, either. Desperate situations made people act in desperate ways. Picturing Jonas' blanched eyes triggered me to shiver again. Even if he'd administered the herbs to Fannie at her request, he would be implicated in murder if those herbs killed her. I slumped a little, tired. The straightforward robbery attempt and shootout was more to my liking. The murky layers of the Amish underworld were more challenging.

I blew out a breath. "Get the autopsy reports done for these fine citizens first, then check back with the lab. I need to know exactly what was in that cup." I turned to Daniel. "Are you up for taking a drive out to the settlement tomorrow morning?"

Daniel hesitated. "Sure, I'd be happy to—as long as we meet at your place tonight."

Bobby's brows shot up before he made an abrupt departure. The feds looked annoyed, but I didn't care. Warm honey spread out in my belly at the velvetiness of Daniel's persuasive voice.

"You have a deal."

10

DANIEL

Ma, unaware of the attempted bank robbery and my involvement in it, was digging in her flower bed with a hoe in hand when I walked up behind her. Later this evening or first thing in the morning, the local drivers would bring the news to the community and people would gossip and wonder about it like everyone else. The Amish got news, only much later than the rest of the world.

With my afternoon shot to hell, I decided to make a trip to the community without Serenity, figuring I might be able to get more out Ma alone. In the morning, she could ask her own questions. That is, if she followed through with our agreement.

I cleared my throat softly to not startle Ma, but she bolted upright with her hands on her chest anyway. Seeing it was only me, she swiped the air in front of her. "*Ach,* what a fright you gave me."

Ma's hands were covered with dirt and there was a smudge on her cheek. Several strands of her thick, gray hair were loose from her white cap. Even with her disheveled appearance and slight body, she was a commanding figure. Possibly it was because she was my mother and I would always feel like a ten year old in her presence. I'd gone nearly fifteen years without her in my life. Our relationship had only been renewed some six months earlier, so it was still awkward at times.

"I see you've enlarged the flower beds. You've been busy," I commented.

Ma's eyebrow rose and her mouth turned down. "I really doubt you came all the way out here to talk about my flowers. What's on your mind, son?"

My heart skipped a beat. It was the first time she'd addressed me as her son since I'd left the Amish. Hearing her say that simple three letter word gave me an amount of satisfaction I wasn't expecting.

"You're right, as usual. I have some questions about the healing ways and Jonas. When I visited with you and Father the other day, you both were vague about your concerns regarding the man."

Ma wiped her hands on her apron and motioned for me to follow her into the house. The late afternoon sun was dropping low in the western sky, turning the slight breeze chilly. I hoped I could have the conversation with Ma before Father returned home from helping my sister's husband plant the back field. I'd called my sister, Rebecca, before I'd left town to check on Father's whereabouts.

I accepted a cup of coffee from Ma and waited while she settled in the chair across from me at the kitchen table. Ma reached out and pushed aside the vase of bright yellow daffodils blocking her view to see me better.

"Go on," Ma urged.

I swallowed. The fact that she'd probably accidentally referred to me as *son* wasn't lost on me. Ma had been devastated when I'd left the Amish to be with an English girl. She'd told me that it was the biggest mistake of my life. I found out a couple of months later she was right, but I was too stubborn to admit it, swallow my pride and return to the plain life. Sometimes I regretted my decision to leave the Amish, other times I was thankful for it.

"Have you ever grown tansy ragwort?" I asked carefully, paying close attention to her eyes as they widened and then recovered.

Ma chuckled. "You really are ignorant of plants, aren't you? Tansy is a weed that you can find at the edge of any field. There's no need to grow it."

"I see." I scratched my chin. "Do the Amish use this weed for medicinal purposes?"

"Of course. I've used it myself as an insect repellant, but it's been years. When *Mammi* was alive, I remember seeing tansy hanging in her storeroom to dry. The plant can be poisonous, especially when it's just cut. After it's dried, it can still be dangerous to work with. *Mammi* was well practiced with herbal remedies and trusted herself to use it when needed."

I searched my mind for a gentle way to ask my question, a way that wouldn't offend Ma's sensibilities.

"Uh, have you ever heard of tansy being used to cause a woman to lose a pregnancy?"

Ma slumped back in her chair and sipped her coffee. I took it as a cue to take a sip of mine. The flavor was strong, the way I liked it.

"Is this about Fannie's death?"

I nodded. "Look, I can't go into details—it's an active investigation, but something came up about the plant and I thought I'd ask you." I took another sip and swallowed. "I remember how you used to treat people's mild ailments with herbs. You're the most knowledgeable person I know and trust about such things. I was hoping you could help me out."

Ma met my gaze with round, moist eyes. She sniffed, collecting herself.

"*Mammi* told me tansy could be used to end a pregnancy. She was also a midwife, you know. Sometimes a woman loses a baby, but it doesn't come out. It will fester inside of her, causing serious illness. Back in those days, our women didn't go to the English hospitals. Sometimes the community healer would be forced to make up a potion to rid the woman's body of the dead child. It certainly wasn't done often, but from time to time it was needed, unfortunately."

"Can you think of any other reason a woman might drink the stuff?"

Ma's mouth puckered. "It will treat worms, but there are much safer remedies available for that." She hesitated. "Irene didn't know about Fannie's pregnancy. It's such a scandal. I can hardly believe the girl would have sinned in that way."

I frowned at Ma. "You know very well that it takes a man and a woman to make a baby. Fannie wasn't alone in her supposed sinning."

"Supposed? Has the outside world bled every inch of morals from your body?" Ma said with disapproval seeped heavy into her words.

There was no point trying to talk to Ma about righteousness. We'd never see eye to eye on the subject. The only thing I could do was try to keep her from becoming angry and walking out. This was too important.

"Even if Fannie sinned, don't you want to know the truth about her death?"

Ma exhaled. "Of course I do. Fannie and the babe didn't deserve that kind of end. If Fannie had lived, there would have been time to ask for forgiveness and make amends. Now there is none."

I leaned in further over the wooden table top. "What do you really know about Jonas Peachey? Father indicated he thought having the man here would harm the community in some way, but he never elaborated." I took a breath. "It's important you tell me what you know about the medicine man."

Ma straightened her back. "The only time I ever used the healing powers was to save your friend Lester. The feeling that came over me was..." She paused. "...not what I expected. *Mammi* had described it to me years before, and I'd watched her heal on many occasions, so it wasn't unexpected. It just..." Ma trailed off.

The light in the kitchen dimmed with the disappearance of the sun. The sky beyond the windows was the hazy gray before nighttime arrived. I felt a chill, and the low light in the room bothered me. Rising, I picked up the matches from the canister on the countertop and lit the gas light above the table, then the one near the sink. The sudden brightness in the room chased away the eerie sensations of the darkness and Ma's words.

When I sat back down, Ma looked at me with a sense of resolve on her round face. "I wasn't sure if whatever power I touched was heaven sent. It didn't feel right, so I never attempted to touch it again."

"What you did saved Lester. How can that be bad?" I asked.

"I don't rightly know, but I didn't want to risk it. Even *Mammi* was reluctant to use the gift. She only healed when the call to do so was greater than the call not to. The problem

I have with Jonas is that he so willingly embraces something that many of us fear to use. Your father feels the same way I do and so does Aaron, but then, he has his own reasons to not trust that man."

"Do you think Jonas had something to do his wife's death?"

Ma tilted her head. "Women die in childbirth. It's not uncommon. It wasn't the fact that it happened that raised our suspicions. It was what Wilma Gingerich told us afterwards that was the most troubling of all."

I searched my memory for the name, which sounded familiar. "Wasn't she the old midwife in our cousins' Ohio community?"

"That's right. She was there the entire time Robyn labored and what she saw was evil," Ma said.

Father picked that moment to walk through the door. "What brings you by, Daniel?"

I looked back at Ma, ignoring Father all together. "What did she see?" I held my breath.

"It's not something I wish to speak of. You can question her yourself," she said with challenging eyes.

"She's still alive? She must be ninety by now," I exclaimed.

Ma nodded. "Ninety-one to be exact. She lives in the same house in the Black Willow." Ma rose from her chair and grasped my hands. "You must bring the sheriff to Wilma. We'll see what an Englisher makes of the story and what she'll do about it."

Ma squeezed my hands tightly. "By the way," she said, "are you going to make an honest woman of the sheriff?"

My eyes bulged and my checks burned.

"Leave him alone, Anna. It's none of our concern who he spends time with. He's an outsider, remember?" father snapped. He jerked his hat from his head and dropped it on the table.

For once, Father's rudeness was more than welcome.

I took the opportunity and stood. "Thank you talking to me, Ma. Don't worry. We'll find out what happened to Fannie and Robyn."

As I stepped off the porch into the crisper evening air, I exhaled.

As difficult as Serenity was being lately, I wondered if I'd just made a promise to my mother that I wouldn't be able to keep. Would Serenity be willing to drop everything to take a trip to an Ohio Amish community to talk to an elderly woman who probably had dementia?

When I climbed into the Jeep, the first thing I did was check the messages on my cellphone.

I couldn't help saying a silent prayer of thankfulness that Serenity had texted me. She was on her way home.

11

SERENITY

My eyes kept drifting to the clock on the dresser. Any minute Daniel would knock on the door. Or perhaps he'd use the spare keys I gave him. I was kicking myself in the butt for giving them to him now. At the time, it seemed like a good idea. Since then, I'd decided never to make any decisions while my clothes were off.

Shutting my laptop, I deposited it on the night table and stared ahead at the rustic wood framed painting on the wall. It was a Christmas gift from Daniel. I frowned at it. There was a black buggy in the driveway behind an equally black horse. The sky was blue and the foliage was thick and green from summertime heat. The cornfield drew my eyes. The tall green plants were crowded together in the bright sunshine, looking happy and harmless, but I wasn't fooled. I would never forget the ominous press of those plants against me as I'd wandered through the field searching for clues to Naomi's death.

It had only been six months ago, but it seemed like an eternity. My heart still clenched at the thought of the pretty girl my nephew had fallen in love with and her tragic end. It was so unfair. All she had wanted to do was escape her tedious life, and she'd died for it.

At least I wasn't having nightmares about saving her anymore. After I'd managed to get there in time to rescue Mariah in the Poplar Spring's community from a drug overdose and Cacey from a crazy ex-Amish drug dealer, I'd found a sort of absolution.

I picked up the piece of paper lying next to me on the bed and read it for the third time.

> *Sheriff Serenity,*
>
> *I write to you with splendid news. I'm heading home today. I've successfully been drug-free for two months. The counselors have released me as being healed. I'm excited to return to the community. I never thought I would miss it, but I did. My parents and Brandy are the only people I've seen from home since I came to this place. Without their support, I wouldn't have made it.*
>
> *I don't know if you've heard about Anna King and Rowan. They're getting married in June. All charges against him were dropped by Sheriff Gentry and he's been able to move on with his life. The sheriff said something to my Da about enough lives being ruined. We had all prayed for such an outcome, especially for Rowan's children's sakes, but never really dreamed it would happen.*
>
> *Other good news is that Jotham left his property and business to Rowan until Rowan's son, Gabe, reaches adulthood. Once Gabe's eighteen, he'll inherit it all. It's unclear why Jotham would have done such a thing, but the income from the store is helping Rowan*

rebuild his barn from the fire. Gabe would have it no other way. Hopefully, without sounding too selfish, the best news is that Gabe has welcomed me to take my waitressing job back if I want it.

For the first time in forever, I'm looking forward to the future. Thank you again for making it possible. I hope to see you soon.
With affection,
Mariah Fisher

I wiped the wetness from my eyes with the back of my hand. The people of Poplar Springs seemed to be enjoying some much needed peace. I thought about Anna, the school teacher and her shy flirting with Rowan and smiled. She had managed to lasso the man after all. Good for her and for all of Rowan's children. They were special kids and so was Mariah. I was surprised that she wanted to remain in the community, but not in a bad way. The simple life might be just what that girl needed.

Depression hit me when I thought about the day's events. I'd killed a man and had to wash another's brains out of my hair. It wasn't that I regretted their deaths. It was more that I was beginning to understand why I'd put off talking to Daniel for so long. My life was screwed up and dangerous. I couldn't act like a normal woman, hoping for all the things that most women wanted. I lived in a world of violence and chaos. My life was in jeopardy at least once a month, even though I wasn't in the big city anymore. I'd discovered the hard way that there were as many sickos living in the country and for some reason, they were to be drawn to me like bees to honey.

I tapped my finger on the pillow, rehearsing what I'd say to Daniel. My throat became dry and itchy at the thought.

Staring at my cellphone, I grunted and picked it up, dialing. "Hello?"

Hearing Laura's voice made me feel better. She wasn't just my only sibling, she was my best friend.

"It's me. What are you doing?"

"Oh, hi, Serenity. I'm just pulling up to the mall to pick up Taylor and her friends. They went window shopping."

"Lucky girls." I paused, glancing at the framed picture on the dresser of Laura, my brother-in-law and my niece and nephew. My family portraits had burned with my house, but Laura had supplied me with more. "How's Will?"

Laura's voice softened. "I talked to him last night for a few minutes. He was getting ready to go into the arena to work cows at a local rodeo. He seems to be enjoying Montana, making friends, but I wouldn't be surprised if he's home by Christmas. I think he's lonely."

I heard the hopefulness in my sister's voice. I wasn't so sure Will would be back that soon. He'd lost the love of his life not too long ago. I figured he wouldn't be back until he met a new girl he liked and really moved on. I didn't voice my thoughts to my sister, though.

"I hope he does..." I trailed off.

"Are you doing okay? When I talked to you earlier, you seemed pretty pumped that only the bad guys were killed in the attempted robbery. Now you sound glum. What's up?"

Leave it to Laura to pick up on my mood. I only wished I could tell her the truth—the real reason I was chewing myself up from the inside out. I wasn't ready yet. It wouldn't be right to talk to my sister about it before Daniel. I owed him that much at least.

"It's a cop thing. I was buzzed on adrenaline earlier. Now I'm sitting here, going through the scene in my head. I guess when the action slowed down, I realized how much danger everyone had been in. In my line of work, things like this happen and you just have to deal with them. There's a steady stream of bad guys fucking up the world."

"You should take a day off. Come over and hang out with me. I just finished last year's accounting for the shop's taxes. We can watch movies. It will be fun," Laura said in a convincing tone.

"Sorry, sounds great, but I'll be wrapped up in paperwork and meetings with the feds all week. There was also a strange death in the Amish community the other day that I'm investigating."

"Another mystery with the Amish, huh? I don't envy you."

"I know. This one's weird. Maybe I'll have time to stop by for dinner over the weekend and fill you in on all the gory details," I suggested.

"I'll look forward to it. Here come the girls. I'll talk to you later, okay?"

"Yep, I'll be around." I hung up.

Daniel peeked around the corner. "Ah, I'm not so sure you will be."

His worried grin made my stomach do a somersault. What now?

"You want me to take a trip to an Amish community in Ohio to talk to a ninety-year-old woman about a death that occurred ten years ago?"

Daniel nodded. He sat on the edge the bed, turned toward me. He'd lost the grin.

"I just had an armed robbery in the Blood Rock Bank with all four assailants shot dead. It made national news. I can't leave town."

I wasn't as perturbed with Daniel as I was with the timing of everything. The opportunity to interview a woman, even an ancient one, about what happened to Robyn Peachey was more than intriguing. It could lead to answers about Fannie's death and Jonas' possible involvement.

"I don't see why not. It's not an ongoing situation. The bad guys are dead, no one else is injured. My construction crew is going to be working the entire weekend to repair the glass and spackle the places in the walls with bullet holes. The bank will be open on Monday. What's the big deal?" Daniel shrugged.

I rolled my eyes and groaned. "There's expectations of a sheriff at times like this." I dared to meet his gaze. "You're right, I'm not specifically needed in town at the moment, but it would look terrible if I suddenly left town."

"Don't you think Fannie Kuhns and Robyn Peachey are worth the trouble?" Daniel challenged.

I took a deep breath to keep myself from shouting at Daniel and counted to five in my head. "Of course, I care. You of all people know how invested I am in learning the truth about mysterious deaths and cold cases, but I'm an elected official. I have assumed obligations to live up to. If I'm not careful, I might not have the position for long."

"I get it." Daniel exhaled. "I guess I'll make the trip on my own, find out what I can and report back to you." He sighed.

A black, stormy cloud settled over me. I wanted to go talk to this midwife myself. Daniel was great at dealing with his people, but he didn't have any detective training. He might say something to Wilma Gingerich that would make her testimony inadmissible in court. And then there was the crazy healing scene that I'd witnessed with Jonas Peachey and Mervin. Strange things were in the wind.

"When did you want to leave?" I inquired, trying to sound disinterested.

Daniel's lips curved for a second and then wobbled as he tried to smooth out his grin. "Tomorrow morning sometime, but I'm flexible."

"Hmm. Perhaps if I go in to the office early, I can get the pertinent reports and files in order. I'll have to check in with Bobby to see if he needs me for anything, and then there's Ed to deal with."

Daniel's teeth flashed. "I don't think the mayor will give you a hard time. After all, you saved his ass this morning."

I leaned back on the pillow. "You were pretty instrumental in saving his ass, too." I took a shaky breath. "You really shouldn't have interfered. You aren't a trained officer and you put yourself and everyone else in jeopardy when you pulled that gun," I said, working hard to keep the tone of my voice neutral. It had been bugging me all day and it felt good to get it off my chest.

Daniel looked like I'd punched him in the face. The room was quiet enough to hear a pin drop. I could hear my heart beating in my ears.

After a long, uncomfortable pause, Daniel said, "You're right. It was foolish. I thought I saw movement through the glass. I knew in my heart you were on the other side of the door. I had faith that together, we'd be successful."

My eyes teared up. I sniffed and quickly wiped the wetness away, but not before Daniel saw. His face scrunched before he crawled up the bed and pulled me into his arms.

I rested there, absolutely still, listening to his heart pounding against my ear. He was warm and solid. Part of me never wanted to let go.

Daniel rubbed my back and nuzzled the top of my head. "We survived. We're all right," he murmured.

He pulled back and I reluctantly looked up at him. "You know we need to talk," he whispered.

I nodded, but didn't move.

"Have you taken a test yet?"

The expectant tension was clear on his face.

"No. I've been a little busy lately." I chuckled nervously.

Daniel sat up straighter. "This is important. You need to do it. I'll run over to the pharmacy right now and bring one back for you. All you'll need to do is pee on the thing."

I took a trembling breath. "I don't think it's necessary. I've been late before. It has a lot to do with the stress of the job. I'll probably wake up in the morning and it will have started."

"Why are you so afraid to take the test? I would think you'd want to know for sure. If you're not pregnant, you can forget about it." He paused, swallowing. "If you are, well, you'll need to go to a doctor for a checkup, make sure everything is all right. After what happened to Fannie, I think it's better to be on the compulsively safe side."

I frowned at him. "It sounds as if you're excited about the prospect of an accidental pregnancy."

"Accidental? There were times when we didn't bother to take precautions. I hardly call it an accident."

Blood rushed to my head, pounding. I sat up straighter. "Wait a minute. Yeah, there were moments when…we…were too preoccupied to be careful, but I'd hardly call it planned. More like stupid."

Daniel's voice hardened. "I never said, *planned*. My point is that neither one of us was overly worried about the consequences, which leads me to believe that we both wanted it."

"You might have. I didn't," I snapped.

Daniel ran his hand through his thick brown hair, pulling on it. He took a calming breath before he spoke.

"It doesn't really matter how this situation came about. We have to deal with it head on. Maybe you're right, and you're not even pregnant. First things first." He climbed off the bed and I panicked.

"Please don't go to the store right now."

Daniel paused, looking back. "It's not a big deal, Serenity. Whatever the outcome from the test is, we'll be all right. I promise."

I inched closer to him with pleading eyes. "Give me a few more days. Honestly, I think it's a waste of your money. I've got too many things on my mind to deal with it. Please."

Daniel shook his head, but said, "Have it your way. But if your period hasn't started in by the weekend, you have to do this. For both of our sakes."

I nodded vigorously and threw my arms around his neck. The scent of his cologne filled my nose. I leaned in and put my mouth on his. He didn't hesitate kissing me back. We sighed into each other's mouths as his hands pressed me closer.

The violence and death of the day slipped away. Daniel was my drug, an addiction I craved more than I cared to admit. I was gloriously safe in his muscled arms.

I pulled my night shirt over my head and Daniel's lips found my breast. I arched, giving him more access as his fingers found my other sensitive place. I wrapped my legs around his waist as his tongue thrust in my mouth. I felt his desire pressing against my belly. Thoughts about Fannie, the robbery, supernatural healings—and a possible baby—still swirled in my head, but those troubles became more distant by the second.

At that moment, I didn't care about anything else—except Daniel.

12

SERENITY

I experienced a strong sense of Déjà vu as I looked out the window at the passing scenery. Sure, the season was different, but I was still driving into a strange Amish community and the unknown. The land was flatter here than Indiana, not a hill in sight. The ground was darker, too. As far as I could see, there were plowed fields waiting for crops to grow. Dotting the sea of dirt was the occasional pristine farmstead. They were all similar, consisting of two story white farmhouses, white barns and silos. These were working farms.

My eyes trained on the yellow road sign with the black silhouette of a horse and buggy ahead. SHARE THE ROAD. A shiver of anticipation ran up my spine when we drove past the sign. *We're almost there.*

"How long has it been since you visited this particular community?" I asked almost absently, looking at Daniel from the corner of my eye.

He was wearing large aviator sunglasses, a gray t-shirt and denim jeans. He hadn't bothered to shave that morning and a dark shadow of prickly hair growth over his jaw was visible. My thoughts began to wander back to the night before when that same jaw had moved slowly over my stomach and then lower. I swallowed and shook my head in an attempt to chase the image from my mind.

"Hmm, it must be about twenty-some years. I was just a kid. As I got older, I didn't travel to visit the family as much anymore."

"Do you still have relatives here?"

"Of course. Probably dozens of cousins. I lost track of them when I left the Amish." He smiled ruefully. "You know, when you're shunned, you don't get any more Christmas cards."

"The Amish send cards for Christmas?"

"Sure, why not?"

"Oh, I don't know. It just seems like sending cards is kind of materialistic in a way," I said lamely.

"Ma used to make her own. I'm sure she still does. I imagine my sister buys a box from the store. Keeping in touch with relatives is important to the Amish, and what better way than at Christmas," Daniel said, slowing to a stop and then turning left.

We passed clusters of wooded islands on each side of the road. The foliage on the trees was turning green, becoming more pronounced. The warm breeze stirring from the narrow opening in the window even smelled green.

"There's a lot I don't know about your people. Even as much as I've been around them the past few months, I'm still completely ignorant about so many things."

Daniel snorted in good humor. "I grew up Amish and I'm still surprised sometimes."

Unwanted thoughts pestered my mind, pushing themselves out my mouth on their own accord. "You know...if I were pregnant, the child would be part Amish."

Daniel shrugged. "It's a neat background to have, I think."

"Maybe," I mumbled, my thoughts wandering again.

"They're not as bad as you think. You've seen my people during some really trying times when they were at their worst. Usually, life is pretty peaceful and quiet. Not at all what you've grown accustomed to."

I looked sideways. "I think it's odd that you still refer to them as *my people*. You're not Amish anymore, remember?"

Daniel's brow lifted above the rim of his sunglasses. "I think most people refer to their home being wherever they grew up. If someone was raised in New York, they don't lose that northern accent and those opinionated mannerisms when they move to Florida. Just the same, a southerner's drawl might soften with time away from home, but never truly disappear. It's the same with me. Growing up Amish shaped me. It's a part of me whether I like it or not," Daniel said quietly.

"Was there ever a time when you *really* wanted to go back?" I faced Daniel, chewing on my bottom lip.

Daniel took a moment to think out his response before he answered, worrying me even more.

"Right after I discovered what a mistake I'd made leaving home to be with an English girl, I regretted my actions, but I was too stubborn to admit it. Those were tough years. I managed to survive. It wasn't until much later that I began to miss the honest living and community spirit of the Amish. It really hit me right before I met you. I was lonely."

I looked back out the window. It was funny how you could see a person almost every day, sleep and eat with him, and still not really know him at all. In so many ways, Daniel was a stranger to me, having basically grown up on another planet.

"You had friends and your work crew—and a string of girl-friends. Most men would be thrilled with such a life," I scoffed.

Daniel laughed. "That's what most men want, except for me. If there's one thing I did take from the Amish, it was the love of family. Ever since I was a young man, I dreamed of having my own wife and children."

"You could have had it several times over if you really wanted," I accused.

Daniel shook his head in frustration. "It's not about having it with just anyone. After Abbey, and until you, I never felt inclined to get serious with another woman."

"And now you're ready for it." I snorted.

"Yes, I'm ready for it, even if you're not." Daniel hit the brakes hard before he turned onto a gravel driveway leading to a small white house beside the road. I lurched forward into the tightening seatbelt.

I didn't say anything. The last thing I wanted was to get into an argument with him before we interviewed the old lady.

I focused on the front porch where a black lab with white fur around his muzzle shuffled down the steps. He barked half-heartedly at us while we got out of the Jeep.

I guessed that the woman sitting in the rocking chair on the front porch was Wilma Gingerich.

She looked even older than I had imagined.

I lifted my chin into the breeze and listened to the chirping of the birds, instead of the unintelligible mumblings between Daniel and Wilma. The type of German that the Amish spoke wasn't taught on learning disks. This was the main reason I'd enlisted Daniel's help with my first Amish investigation.

The *clip clop* of hooves on the pavement drew my gaze down the road. A slick, high-headed black horse trotted by, pulling a buggy. A hand shot out of the buggy, waving at Wilma's house. Both Wilma and Daniel waved back. The sound of the horse's hooves grew fainter, until the countryside was quiet again.

Some bees flying around the forsythia bush at the corner of the porch caught my attention. Watching the bugs dart between the yellow flowers and listening to the incessant drone of their buzzing made me sleepy. Daniel had stayed the night, and because of his insatiable appetite in bed, we'd been up late. The long morning at the department was finally catching up with me. I yawned, closing my eyes.

"Serenity. Wilma is ready to answer your questions," Daniel said, his voice slicing through my fogginess.

My eyes popped open. I took a breath and smiled at Wilma. The crinkles around her eyes deepened as she smiled back at me.

I pulled a little notebook from my pocket. "Thank you for speaking with me on such short notice." I glanced down at my previous notes and back up again. "Is it true you were there when Robyn Peachey gave birth to Esta, a baby girl, about ten years ago?"

Wilma nodded in unison with her rocking. "Yes, ma'am. I was there."

"Did anyone else attend the birth?"

"Ada Mae—and Jonas was there at the end," she said in a quiet, but not fragile voice.

Even though Wilma was of advanced age, her gray eyes were clear. I was pleasantly surprised to get the impression that she probably had the ability to recall things that happened long before Robyn died in childbirth. *Wilma was still as sharp as a tack.*

"Are you saying you and Ada Mae started the birthing process with Robyn, but Jonas finished it?"

Wilma shook her head slightly. "Ada Mae and I were there the entire time Robyn labored. Jonas only arrived right before the baby came out."

"Where had Jonas been?" I asked carefully, hoping not to look too suspicious of the man. I wasn't sure about Wilma's feelings for him.

"He visited one of the local children. She was sick. When he left in the morning, Robyn's pains hadn't started yet, so he went on his way."

"Did the birth progress normally before Jonas arrived?"

"Why yes. It was her fifth child. Her body was accustomed to it." Wilma stared back at me.

I swallowed. "What happened then?"

Wilma took a breath and gazed out at the field running parallel to her yard. There were several brown cows with calves at their sides.

"It is always sad to lose a calf, but to lose the cow is even worse. It was the same with poor Robyn. We were devastated. By the time Jonas arrived, Robyn had been laboring for several hours, longer than I thought a woman with her number of children should have. Ada Mae agreed with me. We allowed Robyn to begin pushing, but the baby just wouldn't drop on its own. Jonas had delivered nearly as many babies as I had. When he arrived, he took charge of the situation." She took another forced breath, turning to Daniel. She said a few sentences to him in German. When he nodded, motioning for

Wilma to continue, she faced me again. "Jonas was suddenly afraid for his wife. He saw something that we had not. Maybe it was the paleness of her skin or something of a vision. He asked Ada Mae to bring the anointing oils, and he laid his hands on her—"

"Exactly how did he place his hands?" I interrupted.

"The same as his grandmother taught him. One hand on the head and the other on the stomach. He began the chanting ritual. A few moments later the baby was born healthy and Robyn was dead."

I glanced at Daniel. His eyes were wide and he was frowning. It wasn't the best timing for this kind of conversation, but I was more concerned that Wilma didn't have any more information for me. There wasn't a lot to go on here.

"Did Jonas do anything with the hand he had on Robyn's stomach?"

"He pushed down as he should have. Sometimes, the child needs to be manipulated with the hands to enter the birth canal."

"Was Esta breach or ill positioned?" I asked, drawing on my small reservoir of knowledge about childbirth.

"She came into the world headfirst," she confirmed.

"Why do you think Robyn died?"

"There was too much blood. She became unconscious. The English doctors couldn't even save her."

"Wait—she was taken to the hospital?"

Wilma nodded. "Jonas had his daughter, Gloria run to the corner phone box. She dialed the emergency number. The ambulance came and took Robyn away."

"Do you have any idea which hospital she went to?" I asked, holding my breath.

"I believe it was the Catholic one—Mercy."

Daniel was already pulling the car keys from his pocket.

I stood. "How was Jonas' behavior?" Seeing the confusion on Wilma's face, I added, "Was he very upset or fairly calm?"

Wilma smirked, sending a tingle racing up my spine. "It's the only time I ever saw that arrogant man cry. Perhaps it was because he failed with the healing—also a first time as far as I know."

I hesitated, trying to formulate the question in a way that wouldn't sound absurd. When I glanced down, Wilma was waiting patiently, reminding me of a cat lounging outside a mouse hole.

I tried to blow off the uneasiness I was feeling. "Are you a healer?"

Wilma laughed. "No, child. I have delivered dozens of babies over the years, but I have no abilities other than knowledge."

I appreciated her honesty. "Do you believe Jonas can heal with his hands?"

"He is a conduit for power. That is all."

"Where do you think the power comes from?" The question wasn't pertinent to the scientific investigation, but I asked it for my own benefit.

She didn't hesitate. "I believe it depends on the person using it. If they are good in the heart, it is from God. If they are evil, then it is the serpent they work with."

The air on the porch grew cooler and I shivered.

Movement and the flash of light blue at the edge of the house caught my eye. I craned my neck to see a woman peeking around the corner. Her cap blended in with the white paint on the house and her dress was the color of a winter sky. She had a long face that resembled Wilma's enough to make me guess they were related. She didn't scurry away. Instead, she stared back at me with round eyes.

"Who's she?" I pointed at the woman spying on us.

Wilma swiveled in her rocker enough to see for herself. "Oh, that's my granddaughter, Marissa." She waved her hand. "Come out Marissa. No reason to hide."

Marissa trotted away from her hiding spot and up the porch steps. She came to a stop in my personal space. I stood my ground, studying the slender woman up close. She appeared to be around thirty. There were fine lines around her dull, gray eyes that were probably brought on from working outside in the sunshine her entire life. Without the benefit of wearing makeup, I could see the blotches and imperfections on her skin from sun damage. Her plain brown hair was free of any gray hairs, though.

"Hello," I said.

"*Hullo,*" Marissa mimicked me, only with a heavy accent.

I looked past Marissa at Wilma. "I think she overheard us."

Wilma swatted the air in front of her. "No worries about Marissa. She has the mind of a five year old. I'm sure she didn't understand much of what we were saying." Her gaze settled on her granddaughter. "Go on, girl. I'm sure those hens have some eggs for you to collect."

A huge smile erupted on Marissa's face. "Cluck, cluck, it's time to get the eggs, time to get the eggs, time to get the eggs," she rambled as she left us. She disappeared around the same corner of the house where I had first spotted her.

I swallowed, recovering from the strange encounter with Marissa. "Thank you again for you time," I said reaching down to shake Wilma's hand. She held onto to my mine longer than necessary, making me feel more uncomfortable.

When she let go, I turned, suddenly wanting to be away from Wilma, Marissa and strange talks of God and serpents. I forced myself to wait on the porch steps as Daniel said his farewells to the old woman in German.

A thought occurred to me and I whirled around, stopping Wilma before she slipped through her front door. "Do you remember if Robyn drank any tea during the delivery or maybe before?"

Wilma looked over her shoulder. "Our women are usually provided tea at birthing. I remember Robyn drinking from a cup."

"What was in the tea?"

Wilma shrugged. "I don't remember. There are many different herbs that soothe the senses and ease the pain of childbirth."

"Do you know any of the herbs that are commonly when a woman is in labor?"

"Lavender or wild lettuce maybe. I know very little about herbs. You should ask Ada Mae. She trained right along with Jonas. Unfortunately, Ada Mae didn't possess the healing gift the way Jonas did. She focused more on the plants and their uses in treating ailments. She might have the answers you're looking for."

I pulled out a business card from my pocket and placed it in Wilma's hand. "If you remember anything else, please call me."

Wilma didn't wait for me to ask any more questions. She disappeared through the doorway, the sound of the screen door thudding shut behind her.

"We have one more stop to make here before we head home," I told Daniel as we climbed into the Jeep.

"I figured as much." Daniel grinned at me, lifting the dreary and almost creepy cloud of feelings that had settled over me while I had talked to Wilma.

I still wasn't entirely sure any murders had taken place, but I knew one thing for sure. What I'd witnessed and felt in Jonas' house when he supposedly healed Mervin was beyond my understanding.

And that scared the hell out of me.

13

DANIEL

I glanced at the ENTERING BLOOD ROCK sign and then at Serenity. I was drained. I had hoped the long drive to and from the Ohio Amish settlement would have given us more time to discuss our future together. But the only subjects Serenity wanted to talk about were Fannie's and Robyn's deaths—and the power of healing. I got it. We were knee deep in the middle of another investigation, but after this one, there'd be another one, and another. I was beginning to doubt whether Serenity would ever put aside her career for her personal life.

"I wonder how common it is for a woman to bleed to death after giving birth," Serenity remarked.

I looked at her. She was staring out the window at the darkening sky.

"You'll have to ask Bobby that one. I have no idea," I replied gruffly.

Serenity exhaled. "Even though we have Robyn's death report," —she waved the paper in the air— "we aren't any closer to knowing whether it was natural causes that did her in or something more sinister. We certainly can't make a direct connection between her death and Fannie's from this."

"It seems like an awful amount of bad luck, if you ask me." Serenity's head snapped my way. "Please elaborate."

"I remember growing up, a lot of the women in the community had babies at home. I don't recall a single death occurring. Either Fannie and Robyn were simply on the wrong side of the percentages or their connection to Jonas somehow contributed to their deaths."

"What is your gut telling you?" she asked, dropping her voice.

I couldn't see her eyes. The sunglasses she wore covered them completely. She didn't need them. The sun had almost set on the horizon. Without the uniform, wearing only faded denim jeans and a blue, zipped up hoodie, she looked like a teenager. I knew she carried a revolver in her purse and had a 9 MM strapped to her side. She was the toughest woman I had ever met, but sometimes, like now, she seemed vulnerable.

"I'm not really sure. It doesn't add up, but there isn't any smoking gun, either." My voice sounded hollow.

"I feel about the same way. There's something bothering me, as if we're not getting the entire picture." She turned towards me, removing her sunglasses. Her blue eyes sparked. "For one thing, why would Jonas kill his wife? He never remarried. He's Amish. It doesn't make sense. As far as Fannie is concerned, maybe she fooled around with a local boy, got pregnant and was terrified of being found out. She's on the plump side anyway, so she was able to hide the pregnancy longer than someone else might have. When she got to the point that she started showing, she might have decided to end the pregnancy using an herb that caused abortion. Case closed."

"That's a good theory."

"*But?*" she replied.

I chuckled. She knew me pretty well. "I don't think she would have had the knowledge to do such a thing. Not only is abortion completely against any Amish person's morals, it's not something they even talk about."

"I was thinking the same thing, which brings me to the conclusion that one of two things happened. Someone helped her abort and in the process, she accidentally died. Or someone, maybe even the baby's father, slipped the stuff into the drink to end the pregnancy. Either way it's manslaughter or murder."

"I'll drive you out to the community in the morning and you can ask some more questions. Bobby might even have the conclusive lab results by then." I paused, taking a breath. "If it's all right with you, I'll stop by my house to pick up some fresh clothes and check my messages. It will be easier if I stay the night at your place."

I lifted the side of my mouth, along with my brow in Serenity's direction. She met my gaze for several long seconds.

"Sounds like a plan to me," she finally replied, avoiding eye contact.

"We can even stop by the drugstore—"

"Don't push it," Serenity said sharply, cutting me off.

I looked straight ahead. She was right. I had to slow down. Serenity wasn't a fool. She'd do it when she was good and ready.

A glimpse of shiny silver caught my attention as I turned into my driveway. I caught my breath, holding it when I saw the car parked in front of my house. I groaned and slumped in the seat.

"Who's that?" Serenity asked, squinting to see the car better.

I swallowed, afraid to say the words. "It's Elayne."

"Why is she at your house?"

I shrugged. "I don't know." I didn't flinch when I met Serenity's stony glare. "Don't get all jealous on me. There's nothing going on between me and Elayne."

Serenity's lips pressed together and her eyes narrowed. "Whatever," she snapped.

I thudded my head against the headrest as I cut off the engine. Serenity's car was parked on the other side of Elayne's. I already knew with dreaded certainty what she was going to do.

"Please, Serenity. Don't make an issue of this," I begged.

Serenity smiled sweetly back at me, not saying a word. She grasped the door handle and was out of the Jeep before I could grab her.

She wasted no time strutting over to Elayne, who stepped out of the car.

"Hello, Sheriff Adams. I didn't expect to see you here with Daniel," Elayne said with a smile that didn't reach her eyes.

"Yeah, well, Daniel is helping me with an investigation," she said with a much calmer voice than I expected.

"Oh, I see." She glanced between me and Serenity. The tension in the air was thickly uncomfortable. Elayne's gaze landed squarely on me. "We kind of got sidetracked after the fiasco at the bank yesterday. I was hoping I could take a look at the apartment, Daniel. I have to rent something quickly," she said with a flip of her long hair. She smiled again, flashing her white teeth.

"It's not a good time. I have—"

Serenity interrupted with a raised hand. "You go on ahead and help Miss Weaver get settled. We want to show our new assistant DA how hospitable we are here in Blood Rock." I opened my mouth to argue and she cut me off again. "Really, I *insist*."

I saw the stubbornness in her eyes before she turned back to Elayne. "Have a nice evening."

She already had her duffle bag and purse slung over her shoulder when Elayne grasped her shoulder. Serenity's eyes dropped to Elayne's hand.

"Wait, I never did get the chance to thank you for risking your life to save us at the bank. You were incredibly brave," Elayne gushed.

"It's my job. I'm paid to be brave," Serenity said.

"Oh, I think it's more than that. I'm looking forward to working with you on cases in the future. We're going to be a great team."

Serenity's eyes widened and a smirk appeared on her mouth for an instant, then it was gone. "I'm sure you're right. Good night, both of you."

When Serenity's stormy eyes met mine, I knew I was in deep trouble.

14

SERENITY

The boxes blurred in front of me. I took another breath in an attempt to slow down my pounding heart. It was kind of ironic. I had the ability to stay perfectly calm in any emergency situation, and yet, here I was, about to have a complete meltdown because Daniel was showing Elayne an apartment.

I need to trust the man, I told myself, but the fact that Elayne was an old Amish acquaintance and drop-dead gorgeous to boot were problems. I didn't think my reaction was completely unjustified. Hell, most women would probably agree that I had a right to be worried and pissed. It didn't matter, though. I wanted to give Daniel the benefit of the doubt and would force myself to be a grownup, but I'd also prepare for the worst.

My eyes skimmed over the pregnancy tests. There were so many different kinds. Some were cheap, others fairly expensive. They all seemed to involve peeing on a stick or in a cup. I glanced around again. The butterflies raging in my stomach had only gotten worse when I'd entered the drugstore. The last thing I needed was for someone to spot me in this particular aisle. I pulled the navy blue ball cap down further on my forehead. I didn't go out much in street clothes. I didn't even own many clothes. I woke up, put on the uniform, worked until dark and traded it for pajamas when I finally got home. If I was quick, no one would notice me with my hair down and the cap shielding a large portion of my face.

When the Amish girl turned into the aisle, I held my breath, turned slightly away, and pretended to study the boxes. She was wearing a green polyester dress, black tennis shoes and a white cap. She stopped beside me and began looking at the same boxes I was.

Damn.

Very carefully, I tilted my head to get a better look at the girl.

I dropped my gaze and turned to leave. Walking around the corner, I stepped into the haircare aisle. The girl would have to walk by to check out at the register. Then I could follow her.

I continued to stand there, feigning interest in the shampoos, waiting. My heart pounded.

When the swish of green went by, I began walking, keeping a discreet distance between us. I stopped and turned to feign looking at a magazine rack when the girl entered a checkout lane. The only item she carried was the pink box.

When I went through the automatic doors, the evening breeze was warm. The parking lot was full of cars. People were wearing shorts. All of this only half registered in my mind. My senses were pinpointed on the girl walking straight backed through the parking lot.

I chose a random car and approached it, digging through my purse for the keys. It was only for show. I was in the perfect position to see the girl get into the backseat of a green mini-van. She wasn't alone. In the front seat were two men. The English driver, an older gentleman with graying hair and a neat mustache, and another man with dark hair and the bluest eyes.

I swiveled away from the van as it rolled past me. Even though I was fairly certain no one noticed me, I continued to hold my breath.

When the coast was clear, I sprinted across the parking lot, jumping into my car. My eyes never left the van as it turned onto Main Street. I controlled the urge to peel from the parking space, figuring that I could easily catch up to the van once I got onto the road.

I pulled onto Main Street and was right where I wanted to be—one car behind the van. I relaxed, taking a large gulping breath.

Not surprisingly, we were heading out of town towards the Amish settlement.

I had all but forgotten the reason I'd gone into the drugstore in the first place. My mind was swimming with only one thing.

Why did Hannah Kuhns, Fannie's little sister, buy a pregnancy test, and then get into the van with Jonas Peachey?

I touched the brakes, slowing down. I couldn't risk being seen. I drove by the Kuhns' farm as Hannah exited the van. In my rearview mirror, I saw the van backing down the driveway.

At least the girl was home. Of course, her sister had died in that same home, I reminded myself.

I jumped in the seat when my phone vibrated. I glanced down at it and saw I had three missed calls and a bunch of text messages from Daniel. I ignored them, returning the call from Todd instead.

"Hey, boss. Are you back in town?" Todd asked

"Unfortunately. What's up?"

"The feds have a few papers for you to sign off on. Can you stop by the department tonight?"

"Yeah, sure, but it'll be a while."

"Why, what are you into?"

"I'm currently in the Amish community. I'll be here a little longer. Just leave the papers on my desk."

"Will do. Need any help?" Todd lowered his voice to a more serious tone.

"Naw, not this time. I'll see you later." I hung up.

I turned into Jonas Peachey's driveway. The van was nowhere to be seen. I'd purposely taken the long way around to the farm to give the medicine man time to get there before me. Since there was no sign of the van, I could only assume that he had somewhere else to go before he returned home.

It worked in my favor and I smiled at my luck.

Darkness had settled over the farm by the time I rapped on the door. A lone bird whistled in the distance and a cow mooed. Otherwise the countryside was broodingly quiet.

The door opened a crack before it flung wide open.

"Sheriff Adams. I wasn't expecting you. Come in," Ada Mae said, ushering me in to the house and closing the door behind me.

I glanced around the room. Esta was at the kitchen table, cutting celery with a large knife that would have been frightening for my sixteen-year-old niece to weld. Verna sat beside her little sister with a knitting hook in her hand and yarn in her lap. Some kind of liquid bubbled to the top of a pot on the wood burning stove. My mouth watered. It smelled delicious.

"If you'll excuse me, I don't want this chicken noodle soup to boil over." Ada Mae left me standing by the door to hurry to the pot and stir it. "Esta, go ahead and drop the celery in. Be careful. It's extremely hot," Ada Mae cautioned, turning her attention back to me. "What brings you by, Sheriff?"

I took a few steps away from the door. The kitchen was brightly lit with several lanterns. It felt rather cozy, different from when Jonas had healed Mervin and the taint of creepiness had crawled all over me.

"I'm sorry to bother you at dinnertime, but I have a few questions. Do you have a moment for me?" I asked.

"Of course. It's no bother at all. Jonas is making his rounds this evening, so he won't be back until later. It's just me and the girls. I hope you'll join us for dinner," she said pleasantly, taking the spoon from Esta and shooing her towards the hallway.

Verna stood up, gathering her knitting supplies in her apron. The teenager smiled at me, then touched Esta's shoulder, mumbling something in German to the girl.

"I'm going to clean my room, but I'll be back soon," Esta promised.

I smiled at the girl's tactics, watching her join her sister and turn the corner. Both girls were striking, with the dark hair and blue eyes of their father. I wondered what Robyn had looked like. Unfortunately, the Amish didn't allow portrait pictures. The only evidence that a person existed after they died were memories and their children.

I sat down on the nearest chair, turning to Ada Mae. "You were there for Esta's birth?"

She continued stirring the soup as she dropped in what appeared to be a pinch of salt. "Why yes, I was." She met my gaze. Her eyes were sad and her back slumped. "I try not to think about it. It was a very difficult time for all of us. Robyn's death was so unexpected."

"What do you think happened?"

Ada Mae sighed heavily and put the spoon down. She sat down in the chair beside me. She seemed defeated.

"It was strange. Everything was going smoothly, except maybe she'd been laboring a little too long. After Esta came out, Robyn was bleeding much heavier than she should have been. Jonas became alarmed and sent Gloria to call for help." She shrugged and met my gaze. "Sometimes there are complications during childbirth. I remember my *Mammi* Lily delivering twins when I was only a young girl. The mother died a couple days later from an infection. Nobody knew for sure why she became sick. Robyn's story is similar. Even the doctors at the hospital couldn't give us a specific reason for her loss of so much blood."

Ada Mae's voice had a calming quality to it. If she weren't Amish, I could easily picture her working as a nurse. There was just something about her easy-going manner that reminded me of Todd's fiancé, Heather. She was an Emergency Room nurse.

It was more than likely impossible to find out exactly what caused Robyn's death ten years earlier. Even the doctors at the hospital where she was taken were vague in their answers, feeling that the fact she was Amish and hadn't had any prenatal care with a professional had probably contributed to her death in some way. I'd been told that the original doctor who had tried to save her life was now working in California, and his notes agreed with the coroner's conclusion. I was beginning to feel like I was chasing a ghost.

Changing gears, I took a chance. "It's come to my attention that Jonas was treating Irene before her daughter's death. Do you know anything about this?"

Ada Mae nodded. "He was treating Fannie, too. Ever since Irene's husband passed away from cancer, the Kuhns' women were having issues sleeping at night. I prepared a special chamomile tea to help them rest."

Her words sparked a memory of my earlier conversation with Wilma. "Besides the chamomile, were there other ingredients in the tea?"

"I added a small amount of wild lettuce. It works well with the chamomile to soothe a person's mind, and it helps relieve Irene's asthma. The peppermint makes it taste better. It's my special ingredient."

"Does Jonas know as much about these plants as you do?"

Ada Mae smiled, shaking her head. "Not so much. Even he admits that."

I heard the girls' footsteps coming down the staircase, combined with giggling.

A gunshot blast sounded as the window beside the front door shattered. The girls screamed and Ada Mae exclaimed something in German.

"Get down." I motioned to Ada Mae before I turned to the girls standing in the door opening from the hallway. "On the floor!" I ordered.

I had my gun in hand and was up against the wall in a fluid movement. Adrenaline rushed through my veins as I peeked out into the darkness through the window opening. The farm had no yard lights, my view obstructed by the murkiness of nighttime and shadows stretching down from the barn. I held my breath. There was silence.

The gunning of the car's engine was like a slap to my face. I grabbed the handle of the front door and flung it open. I tried to jog a few times a week, so I wasn't in terrible physical shape, but I hadn't had to rundown a criminal in a while.

The rear lights of an older model sedan disappeared around the bend as I reached my car. I shoved the key into the ignition and flung the car into reverse. *Thunk, thunk, thunk.*

"Dammit," I growled, putting the car into park and jumping out. The back tires were flat. I could see the slashes.

Ada Mae was hesitant as she approached me. The two girls were peeking out the front door.

"Do you have any idea who shot at your house?" I asked, pulling the cellphone out of my pocket.

Ada Mae shook her head. Her face was pale and her mouth gaped open.

I focused on my phone, realizing that the woman wasn't in the proper state to have a conversation.

"Todd, put out an APB county wide for a dark colored, four-door sedan," I said into the phone.

"Is that all you got? Where are you?" he replied, his voice tense.

"That's it. I'm going to need a ride. I'm out at Jonas Peachey's farm in the Amish settlement. It's on the east end of Burkey Road, not too far from where Naomi was shot."

"Got it. I'll let dispatch know. Do you need any personnel—medical help?"

"No. We're good here," I said curtly, hanging up.

The pounding of hooves on the pavement echoed and I raised my head. A horse and buggy blended into the night, but I could follow their approaching movement by sound alone. When the buggy turned into the driveway, the definition of the horse became clear. I glanced at Ada Mae who took the few steps to stand beside me.

Jonas' pale eyes shone out from the buggy before I saw his features. The sight of those freaky eyes made my heart rate speed up again.

Jonas pulled the horse down from a trot to stop beside us. He nodded at me. "I wasn't expecting you, Sherriff. What brings you by?"

My eyes narrowed as I stared at the man. His hair was messy and the top few buttons on his blue shirt were unbuttoned, allowing me to catch a glimpse of black hair on his chest. I gauged his age to be somewhere around forty-five, but he had the swagger of a younger man.

"I wasn't expecting to see you in a buggy, Mr. Peachey," I said. When his brows rose, I took a breath and stopped myself from giving too much away of what I'd seen earlier. "When I was driving over here, I got turned around and ended up on Route Ten. I could have sworn I saw you riding in a minivan," I lied.

"Yes, you probably did. Benjamin, one of the drivers, picked me up from Joseph Bender's farm this afternoon to run errands in town with a couple other community members." He smiled with a shrug. "It's cheaper to pool our resources and share the cost. I left the horse and buggy there until I returned."

Was the guy that smooth or was he telling the truth? It was hard to tell. His eyes were locked with mine, displaying either honesty or intense dominance. His story did make sense, though.

"*Da*, you won't believe what happened," Verna called out from the house. An instant later, she ran up to her father with Esta chasing after her.

Jonas lost the smile and his eyes widened in alarm. He shifted the handle of the buggy into park and hopped out in front of Ada Mae.

"What's happened?" he asked her. His voice rose to a higher pitch.

Ada Mae replied to Jonas in their language. I could only guess from the excited inflections in her voice and her finger pointing at the front of the house, she was telling him about his window being shot out.

When she finished speaking, Jonas turned back to me. "Did you see who did this?"

"It was a navy blue or black, four-door sedan that sped away. I don't believe they fired the shot from the car, either." I motioned to my own car. "Slashed my tires. They were smart enough to do it as insurance that I wouldn't pursue them."

"You keep saying *they*. Did you see more than one person?" Jonas asked.

"No, I didn't see anyone. It's just a feeling, I guess," I answered truthfully, staring at my deflated tires.

"I have an idea of who might have done this," Jonas said slowly.

I met his gaze and he didn't look away. "Go on," I urged.

"Joseph's son has had a couple of run ins with a group of rowdy English teens. That's why I was there. He wanted to talk to me about it," Jonas said.

I tilted my head. "Do you mean the Joseph Bender who's married to Katherine?"

"Yes, that's the one."

"Is it Eli who's having these problems?" I asked. When I said the name, my heart fluttered. He was the boy who was originally courting Naomi before she decided to run off with my nephew. I knew Amish communities were small worlds, but this was ridiculous.

Jonas nodded. "It seems these boys forced his buggy off the road the other night. Luckily, Eli was only bruised. The horse needed stitches and the buggy a new wheel, though. There was another incident where the same boys shoved Eli at the stockyard during an auction."

All the information swirled around in my head like a mini tornado. What any of this had to do with the broken window behind me or Fannie's death, I had no idea.

"Why would Joseph call you and not the bishop or even Moses Buckner? Better yet, here's a novel idea—why not report these incidents to my office?" I crossed my arms in front of me.

"One of the boys is Benjamin's son. Joseph asked me to talk to the man about the situation before we called you. Aaron and Moses are aware of what's going on." Jonas leaned forward in a conspiratorial way. "My people like to govern themselves."

I snorted. I was already aware of how the Amish took matters into their own hands. I heard the cruiser slowing down before I saw it pull into the driveway. I was grateful that Todd didn't come roaring in with the sirens blaring. The horse stomped and looked over its shoulder at the approaching vehicle.

"Girls, please take Remington to the stable and unhitch him. I'll be there shortly to help brush him down," Jonas told his daughters. He turned to Ada Mae. "I have a few bags in the buggy. You can take them to the house."

Ada Mae and the girls went to work, leaving me waiting alone with Jonas while Todd parked beside my car.

"It's nice that your sister is here to help you raise your younger children," I commented.

Jonas puckered his lips. "Yes, I'm blessed to have Ada Mae. I don't know what I would have done without her following my wife's passing."

The car door slamming shifted my gaze from Jonas to Todd. He strode purposely towards us.

"I put the APB out. Haven't heard anything yet. With that kind of a vague description, we're not working with much," Todd said. He came to a stop in front of us.

I introduced the two men and explained to Todd what had happened.

"What's the game plan, boss?" Todd asked me. Jonas appeared to be waiting patiently, but his piercing gaze betrayed him. Those light blue eyes sparked with intensity.

"I guess it's not too late to have a talk with Eli Bender," I said.

"Oh, man. You're kidding me," Todd exclaimed.

"I wish it was a joke," I said.

I'd discovered on the job a long time ago that the same people had a tendency to keep popping up in criminal investigations, so I wasn't as surprised as I should have been.

"I'll have a tow truck out here tomorrow morning to get my car," I told Jonas over my shoulder.

Jonas acknowledged my statement with a lopsided smile. "I hope you find the answers you're looking for, Sheriff."

I didn't look back. Chills crawled over me at his words.

14

DANIEL

"This is perfect. Should I write you a deposit check to hold it for a couple of weeks until I move in?" Elayne asked.

Her voice broke through the haze I'd been in since Serenity had driven away. I looked warily at the brunette. She changed a lot since she'd left the Amish. In those days, she was quieter, more likely to listen than to chatter like a magpie. Looking at her made up face, short skirt, and cleavage-revealing blouse, it was hard to believe she had ever been Amish. Funny. Serenity didn't wear makeup and had her hair in a ponytail most of the time and she was raised on the outside.

I shook my head. "Don't worry about it. I'll hold it for you. We can catch up on the paperwork when you've moved in."

"You're so sweet, Daniel." She tilted her head. "You know, I was a little worried about moving back here, being so close to the community. Having you around is making it easier."

I recognized the longing look on her face. I had to put an end to whatever crazy thoughts were going through her head.

I wanted Serenity. I wasn't going to do anything to make her lose faith in us.

Swallowing, I blew out a breath. "It's been nice to see you, too, but I want to be up front. Serenity and I are dating. I'm very content with the relationship. I'm not going to be able to hold your hand while you readjust to living in Blood Rock. It just wouldn't be right. I hope you understand."

Elayne's mouth thinned into a tight smile. She laughed and swatted my arm. "I thought something was up between you two. I'm kind of surprised though."

"Why?" I dared to ask.

"Well, Serenity is a beauty, no doubt, but she's so, how do I put it without being rude? I guess overly serious is the best way to describe her. When we were kids, I remember you being outgoing and fun—a party guy."

"Serenity is serious because of her job. Every day, she puts her life on the line and she knows the officers who work with her are doing the same thing. She's seen horrible things. She's always thinking and she's ready for anything. She is unlike any woman I've met before and that's why I love her."

"Love? I didn't see that kind of closeness between you two earlier. Forgive my frankness, but she seemed angry at you." She dropped her voice as if she didn't want to say the words. I wasn't fooled.

She was playing the game. I'd been a bachelor a long time. I knew all the games, but I didn't want to give Elayne the satisfaction of knowing her presence in Blood Rock was part of the problem. "All couples have bumps in the road. We're no different," I replied.

"If you ever need to talk about it, I'm here for you. I just hope that Serenity isn't the jealous type. After all, we are old friends." She shrugged and gave a pouty smile. I had to give her credit. A lesser man would be a goner. She was good.

"I don't think it will come to that." I glanced at my watch. "I'm out of time. I'll lock up and you can text me when you're ready to move in. I'll meet you with the key and the paperwork then."

"Yes, I have to go, too. I'm driving out to the settlement this evening," she said, repositioning her purse on her shoulder.

Her words stopped my step. "Are you visiting family?"

"No." She laughed. "I'm not ready for that reunion just yet." She sobered, meeting my gaze. "Do you know Irene Kuhns?"

"Yes, I do," I said.

"One of her daughters died the other day. I guess it was a complication of childbirth. She wasn't even married. Quite the scandal." Her brows arched. "Well, I used to be close to Irene. She has asthma and when I was a teenager, I'd go to her house to clean and do laundry. Her daughters were babies then. Irene was always kind to me, even when everyone else frowned at my rebellious ways. I can only imagine the pain she's going though. I heard she lost her husband last year and now to lose a daughter. I want to check in on her and see if she needs anything."

"Would her surviving daughter, Hannah, remember you?" I asked, feeling the tingle of hope that Elayne might be the way to get Hannah to open up about what had been going on with her sister.

Elayne shook her head. "No, probably not. When I left the community for good, she was a toddler." Her eyes brightened and she leaned in. "Why do you ask?"

Elayne was an intelligent woman and she was going to be the town's assistant DA. I was betting that she'd be willing to help out with the investigation. Serenity wouldn't like it, but how else were we going to get any answers about a shy Amish girl like Fannie Kuhns? Elayne might be our best bet.

I ignored the chalky dryness in my mouth. I wasn't betraying Serenity—I was trying to help her.

I cleared my throat. "Some of the Amish in the community think that Fannie's death might not have been natural."

"Seriously?" Elayne's eyes widened.

"I can't talk to you about who they are and why they have their misgivings. I need you to trust me. If you're up to it, you might even be able to assist the investigation."

Elayne flipped her long hair over her shoulder and grinned. "How intriguing. As long as we stay within the boundaries of the law, you can count me in."

A knot grew in my gut at her quick offer to help. I hoped Serenity would understand.

"It's a long shot, maybe Irene or Hannah will open up to you. I'll wait here in your car."

"If everything you told me is correct, Serenity might have a good case against Jonas Peachey. The situation is certainly questionable," Elayne said with a more serious tone than she'd used since she'd returned to Blood Rock. Having someone in the DA's office who knew the Amish on a personal level, but also understood the law, could be a valuable asset.

"Our people are different. They try to police themselves, and sometimes it just doesn't work out. I hope I'm wrong about my suspicions, but if I'm not, that guy needs to be locked up."

"I agree." Elayne paused, lifting one of her perfectly curved brows. "Wish me luck?"

"You got it," I said, forcing a smile.

I watched Elayne walk in her high heels through the grass and up the front porch steps. She rapped on the door; it opened and she slipped in. It appeared we already had some luck handed to us. There weren't any buggies parked in the driveway and only a couple of windows illuminated dull light.

The moon was full and high in the sky. It had taken longer to show the apartment to Elayne than I had expected, and she'd insisted on getting dinner from Nancy's before we left town. I only agreed if she grabbed a takeout bag instead of dining in. The last thing I needed was for it to get back to Serenity that I'd shared another meal with Elayne.

She'd complained that it was impossible to eat a salad and drive her car at the same time. It was a valid point and I'd offered to drive while she ate. She'd agreed, making me wonder if it was a bad idea. I'd shaken the feeling off and headed out of town with my foot resting heavily on the accelerator. If I was with Serenity, she'd have ordered a burger bigger than the one I was eating, and she would've had no trouble finishing it off while pursuing a criminal at high speed.

I looked out the open window at Irene's vegetable garden. With the moonlight brightening the night, I could make out the shapes of tomato plants stretched neatly in a line. The other plants were still too small to know what they were from this distance, but I guessed she had some sweet corn, green beans and summer squash.

The temperature was warm for this late in the day and this early in the season. I wondered if it signaled an early arrival of summer. I rested my arm out the window as my thoughts strayed to Serenity. With my other hand, I picked up my cell phone again. No new messages. I'd texted her a dozen times since I'd last seen her and she hadn't responded. Under the circumstances, it could be that she was still pissed at me, but I couldn't shake the feeling that something else might be going on. The little sheriff had a way of getting herself into sticky situations. I was half tempted to call Todd and see if she'd checked in with him. The only thing that made me hesitate was that I hated to give the deputy the satisfaction of knowing I didn't have a clue where she was.

My pride was bending, though. If I didn't hear from her in the next ten minutes, I would make the call.

I glanced back at the house. I couldn't see anyone through the windows. I imagined that Irene was making tea and the women would be chatting for a while. Elayne had urged me to drive over to my parents' house or even my sister's while I waited, but I wasn't so sure I wanted to. My mind was heavy with thoughts of Serenity and how to get her to trust me. I was also thinking about the possibility of a pregnancy. A smile tugged at my lips. I couldn't admit it to Serenity, but secretly, the idea of having a child with her was welcomed. In the past, I never took any chances in that department, but with Serenity, I hadn't been as compulsively careful about protection. For the first time in my life, I was all right with the idea of a particular woman having my child. The irony of the situation was that unlike all my other girlfriends, who would have loved to have gone to that level with me, Serenity wanted none of it. Not a baby or a husband or maybe even a life together.

I sighed and thudded my head against the headrest. *Why did Serenity have to be so damn difficult?* Like the previous hundred times I'd asked, no answer was forthcoming.

When the white police cruiser flashed by my peripheral vision, I whipped my head around. The car's sirens weren't on, but it was moving at a fast clip for the Amish roadways where a horse might be pulling a buggy at a two miles an hour walk around any corner.

Without much thought, I started the engine and backed up. Elayne would assume I'd changed my mind about visiting relatives. Keeping the cruiser in my sights, I pulled out of the driveway and accelerated to match its speed.

My heart pounded when the cruiser turned into Jonas Peachey's farm. I rolled to a stop, trying to collect my thoughts. It wouldn't look good if I drove up in Elayne's car. Serenity would wring my neck for sure. I had to explain everything to her about Elayne's connection with the Kuhns family and her willingness to pry a little into what was going on with Fannie, but this wasn't best time to do so.

While I hesitated, deliberating what to do, I noticed a car that looked suspiciously like Serenity's parked in the driveway. My gaze narrowed on the small group standing beside a buggy. Todd walked up to Serenity, who was standing with Jonas and Ada Mae.

I waited a moment more on the quiet road before I lost all patience. I pulled into the driveway as Serenity and Todd were about to get into the cruiser.

Pulling alongside the police car, I hung out the window. "Is everything all right?"

Todd's mouth lifted in the usual smirk. Serenity glared at me.

"I see you and Elayne are now sharing a vehicle. How sweet," Serenity said, causing Todd to snort.

"Let me explain—"

"We're kind of busy here investing a shooting. I don't have time for you."

"Someone was shot?" I thrust the gear in park, flung open the door and leaned into the cruiser, close enough to smell Serenity's vanilla perfume.

Serenity didn't answer, narrowing her eyes.

Todd cleared his throat. "Just barely. Someone shot out one of Mr. Peachey's windows. Serenity was in the house at the time, talking to the man's sister."

I looked back at Serenity now facing forward, ignoring me. "Are you okay?"

"Never been better," she quipped.

"Do you have any idea who did it?"

"It's really none of your concern." She faced me. "You're not a cop, remember?"

I ignored the comment and raised my gaze to Todd. His eyes were wide and cautious.

"If you're going to talk to any of the Amish around here, I can be of service. You both know that," I pressed.

"He has a point—" Todd began.

"We can take care of it." Serenity growled, turning her wrath on Todd.

Todd held up his hands in mock fear. "Okay, okay. You're the boss. If I remember correctly, Daniel does have a relationship with the Bender kid."

Serenity rolled her eyes.

"Eli? You think Eli Bender did this?" I asked, my voice rising.

Serenity blew out an agitated breath, but answered me anyway. "No, not Eli. Jonas mentioned that Eli has been having run ins with some of the local English kids. He believes these kids might be the same ones who popped his window."

I absorbed the information. "Joseph would be more comfortable allowing Eli to talk to you if I was there. Especially after everything that happened during Naomi's investigation," I said as gently as I could.

Serenity's eyes narrowed further. "Eli's over eighteen. His father can't keep us from questioning him, and he isn't a suspect in this case—he's the victim. I think we can handle it on our own."

"Please let me help you, Serenity. You don't understand the way the Amish family system works. As far as Joseph is concerned, Eli won't be an adult until he's married. Even if there's no reason for secrecy, he'll be leery of allowing Eli to talk to you. You know how the Amish are. They like to deal with issues on their own."

"That's what I'm afraid of. If these English kids are responsible for shooting at a house, they've committed a felony. Who knows what they might do next." Serenity lifted her chin, looking into my eyes. "I have to find out what's going on around here and how it all fits together. Do you understand that?"

"I do. That's why you need my help," I insisted.

Serenity glanced at Todd, who shrugged. Her gaze rested on me. "All right, but you're going to have to follow." She motioned for Todd to leave and he put the cruiser in gear and rolled by me.

I hurried back to the Elayne's car and followed them.

I wasn't sure if I was more nervous about being around Serenity in her current mood or about questioning Eli Bender.

Either option wasn't likely to be pleasant.

15

SERENITY

"Have you seen what an outrageous flirt that woman is?" I worked hard to keep my voice level. "Don't take this the wrong way, but she doesn't have to flirt," Todd said with a chuckle.

"Men are all dogs." I sucked in an angry breath and looked away.

"Looking isn't the same as touching. Like I said before, I wouldn't trade Heather in for that high maintenance woman with a bag of cash thrown in." Todd graced me with a slight smile. "I don't think Daniel would trade you, either." He huffed. "Unless you give him no choice, that is."

I dragged my gaze from the blur of the shadowed cropland to gape open mouthed in Todd's direction. "What are you talking about?"

"Hey, I'm on your team here. Don't doubt that. I'm a lot more observant than you might give me credit for. That guy back there," —Todd thumbed behind him— "is crazy about you. He puts up with your job and all the shit that comes with it. He's been thrown together with this new DA by chance.

That's all it is. Trust the guy." He eyed me. "If he fucks up, then kick him to the curb. Not before."

I frowned. Todd was sarcastic, but he cared. He had a little bit more wisdom swirling around in that muscle brain of his than I gave him credit for. Maybe he was right.

"It's so damn hard to have faith after what I went through with Denton, and Daniel is like Denton in some ways. They're both too good looking for their own good and they know it."

"Denton is a shit. He's always been one. I remember him in high school. He had the prettiest girl in the school on his arm, but he wasn't satisfied. I don't understand why you stayed with him as long as you did," Todd growled.

I couldn't stop the smile from lifting on my mouth. "You think I was the prettiest girl in the school?" I teased.

His cheeks reddened. "You already know that. Don't go begging for another compliment."

"No, I didn't," I muttered.

"I was too intimidated to ask you out back then. That goon, who we all knew was screwing around on you with everyone, including your best friend, was always there."

"You weren't too afraid to tease me any opportunity you got," I accused.

"Don't you know that's what guys do when they're sweet on a girl?"

I smiled out the window.

After a moment of reflective silence, I mumbled, "Because I was too trusting—and my pride."

"What?"

"That's why I stayed with Denton for so long," I admitted. I could hardly say it out loud without feeling the same pain of betrayal I'd felt all those years ago stabbing me in the heart.

"I wasn't a huge fan of Daniel, you know that. He's dated almost every pretty woman in the county, making me believe he was a Casanova-type, but since I've gotten to know him better..." He shrugged. "I've changed my mind. He's not your old flame, Denton. If you don't give him a serious chance, you'll more than likely regret it someday."

I pressed my lips together, understanding what he meant. "Turn here. This is the place."

Approaching the farmhouse on the hill raised an army of butterflies in my belly, making it possible to push thoughts of Daniel aside.

I licked my lips, preparing for more Amish shenanigans.

I sat at the kitchen table across from Katherine Bender with a mug of deliciously strong coffee cradled in my hands. Only crumbs remained on the plate in front of me. A few minutes earlier there had been a large piece of peanut butter pie resting there. I was still savoring the sweetness of it on my tongue.

"Do you care for another piece?" Katherine asked with a knowing smile. She was a beautiful woman, on the same par as Elayne, except Katherine wore no makeup and she didn't seem concerned with the few gray hairs mixed in with the brown at her temples. She had porcelain white skin and blue eyes. The baby girl sitting on her lap was quite a bit larger than the last time I'd seen her, and she stared up at me with a drooling mouth. The child favored her mother right down to the milky complexion and brown curls.

I wanted another piece of pie and Katherine knew it. I swallowed hard and gathered all my self-control. "I'm tempted, but I better not. It was excellent, though."

Katherine leaned over the table, resting her chin in her hand. "I'm glad to see that you're still with Daniel. You two are a handsome couple."

With anyone else, I would have snorted, but Katherine was genuinely a nice person. I believed she meant it.

I heard the soft drone of Pennsylvania German behind me in the sitting room. Daniel was sitting in a chair in front of Eli and Joseph, Eli's father, was beside him. Todd was standing over the scene, having no more clue than I did to what was being said. I didn't have trouble trusting Daniel as a translator. He'd proven his loyalty in that department. It was Elayne I didn't trust him with.

Leaving the questioning to Daniel, I met Katherine's gaze. Maybe it was the full belly or the aroma of coffee drifting into my nose. I can't say for sure, but for the first time in forever, I wanted to talk to a woman. Laura didn't count. She was just a sister.

"It hasn't always been easy," I admitted.

"Nothing ever worthwhile is. Especially love." Katherine smiled.

I felt the heat spreading across my cheeks. "Do you by any chance know a woman who used to live in this community by the name of Elayne Weaver? She'd be about your age."

Katherine's eyes grew round as she sat up straighter. The baby squealed at her sudden movement. "Why of course I do!

We were friends before she left us. I heard some time ago that she went onto college and became a lawyer of all things."

"Yep, that's the one I'm talking about. She's moving back to Blood Rock to take on the position of Assistant District Attorney for the county." I watched closely for her reaction to the news.

Katherine leaned in again, the expression on her face darkening.

"Are you certain of this?"

"Oh, yeah. Most certain."

"That's very…nice," she fumbled with the words and stared across the kitchen at nothing.

This wasn't the reaction I expecting.

"I'm sorry. I was just wondering what you knew about her. I met her for the first time the other day and since I'm going to be working with the woman, I was hoping to get the inside scoop on her personality."

"She's here now?" she asked in a shrill whisper.

"Yes," I whispered back, not sure why we were lowering our voices. "As a matter of fact, Daniel's driving her car right now." When Katherine's mouth dropped open, I realized that I really liked her. "Elayne has made sure to reacquaint with Daniel. She's renting an apartment from him, too." I tried not to sound too bitter, but failed.

Katherine placed her hand on mine and tugged me closer across the table. "You must keep an eye on that one," she warned. "She nearly took my Joseph away from me before we were married."

"*No.*" The word slipped from my mouth before I could stop it.

Katherine nodded. "Yes, she did, *and we were friends.* At least I thought we were. I was blessed that Joseph didn't fall for her charms. He picked me. That was shortly before she left the community." She continued to whisper. "I think his rejection of her was part of the reason she left, but I don't know for sure."

Katherine released my hand and I took a swig of my coffee. As soon as I swallowed, I leaned in, resting my chin on my hand. Katherine was waiting for me, mimicking my action. "Were Elayne and Daniel ever an item?"

Katherine shook her head. "Oh, no. He didn't like her much if I remember correctly. He was the one who told Joseph what a fool he was being to risk losing me. I was so thankful that he spoke to Joseph." Katherine grinned. "No worries about Daniel. He has eyes for only one woman—and that's you."

I couldn't help smiling back at Katherine, feeling the tightness of a bond developing. "Maybe I will have that second piece of pie," I said.

"I think I will too." Katherine giggled, pushing her chair back.

"You're going to have to eat it in a hurry," Todd said, stepping up to the table with a frown.

"What do you have?" I asked, standing quickly and snatching my hat off the table.

"The names of a few teenagers that I've dealt with before. This trip wasn't a waste of time," Todd said.

Daniel was saying his goodbyes to Joseph and Eli, and I turned to Katherine. "Can I get a raincheck for that pie?"

But Katherine was already holding out a dish with two pieces of pie neatly wrapped in clear plastic. "For you and Daniel to share later on," she said, grinning.

Now I knew this woman could be a true friend. "Thank you," I mouthed, taking the plate from her hands.

When the door closed behind me, I took a deep breath. The smell of hickory permeated the air. I glanced over my shoulder at the spiraling tendrils of smoke rising from the Bender's chimney. The sharp, homey scent cleared my mind. For the first time in hours, I could look at Daniel without glaring.

"What did Eli say?" I asked.

Daniel looked grim. "It seems that there's a group of English teenagers Eli started hanging around with. He met them at the stockyards one day a few months ago and they hit it off at first. The elders didn't like the blossoming friendship, fearing it might rip Eli and some of the other Amish boys away from the fold." Daniel shook his head, looking at the ground. "So the elders did what the elders do and forbid Eli from hanging around with the Englishers anymore." Daniel jutted his chin toward Todd, who stood with his hands folded in front of him. "Todd knows these kids. They're rough. They've gotten into trouble before. When they heard Eli wasn't allowed to hang out with them any longer, they took it personally. They've been harassing Eli relentlessly over the past few weeks."

I looked at Todd for confirmation. "Yeah, I know these guys. Ethan Rent is eighteen. He's been charged with DUI and drag racing. The judge was lenient with him. He only had community service. Davie Connors and Otis Green are both seventeen. I've had them in on everything from shoplifting, an assault in a parking lot and vandalism at the Lutheran church on Main Street. Both kids served some time in juvie." Todd took a breath. "It's the older one, Arlo Thomas who worries me. I arrested him on domestic violence last year. He punched his mother in the face when she found his stash of weed and flushed it down the toilet. He's twenty-one-years old. One of those grown men who likes to hang out with the young'uns on the weekends."

I glanced at my watch and digested what Daniel and Todd had said. "Do we have any hard proof these guys are the ones who shot out the Peachey's window?"

"Naw." Todd shook his head.

I faced Daniel. "Is Eli willing to press charges against this crew for running his buggy off the road?"

Daniel sighed. "I don't think so. He's hoping things will settle down and get back to normal if he leaves it alone. The Amish don't get involved in the English legal system unless they absolutely have to or they're forced into it."

"Then we don't have squat to go on. All this is hearsay. No witnesses, no evidence." A little flame of hope flared. "Did you get descriptions of their cars?"

Todd answered me. "Otis drives a red pickup truck and Davie Connors, an old SUV. Ethan is on suspended license, so he's not even supposed to be driving, but I'll check up on that. Arlo's family's yard is littered with cars. I seem to recall a darker sedan in the mix, but there are a lot of cars out there that match that description."

"See what you can find out about those vehicles first thing in the morning," I told Todd before I tilted my head to Daniel. "Thanks for talking to Eli. What you got out of him was better than nothing." I forced my face to remain neutral. "Todd will drop me off at home. You can do whatever you need to do with Elayne."

Done talking, I turned to leave, but Daniel reached out, grabbing my arm.

"You should come with me to talk to Elayne—to see what she found out from Irene and Hannah." He frowned. "Unless you're dropping the case," Daniel challenged in a low voice.

I stared into Daniel's dark brown eyes. I could see the spark of desperation there. He wanted to make things right. I could feel the pulsating strings between us, and I wanted things to be right. Should I listen to Todd and Katherine? Were they correct about Daniel's virtue?

I wasn't ready to let it go. The tug of tiredness was making my eyelids heavy. I wanted this night to end, but I didn't want to pass up an opportunity to find out what really happened to Fannie, either. I might be stubborn, but the job came first.

"All right. I'll go with you to talk to Elayne, but that's it." I pointed at Daniel. "You're dropping me off at my place and then you're heading back to yours. I've had a long day and I'm not in the mood for anything else tonight."

I caught a glimpse of Todd's raised brows before he gripped the door handle and got into the cruiser. "Tomorrow, boss," he called out, then cranked the engine.

When I looked back at Daniel, he made a wide sweep of his hand towards Elayne's car. I strode to the vehicle and got in.

We rode in silence over the empty country roads, which suited me fine.

I was having a difficult time concentrating on all the cases. I still had the aftermath of the bank robbery to deal with, and now it sounded as if I had a group of punk-ass young men terrorizing the Amish on my plate. I wasn't sure what to think about Fannie Kuhns, after my interactions with the Peachey family and witnessing a miraculous healing, I was beginning to wonder if I was in over my head with that case. There wasn't any proof of foul play in her death. Sure, it was weird and untimely, but it could have been natural, perhaps exacerbated by the use of clashing herbal remedies.

I rubbed my forehead as we pulled up to the Kuhn's residence.

The only bright spot of the evening was seeing the look of complete shock on Elayne's face when she saw me sitting in the front seat of her car.

Her red cheeks and dark expression when I didn't get out to accommodate her was priceless. The fact that she hadn't gone to the driver's side to displace Daniel first was her undoing. He remained planted in his seat, even after she finally glanced his way. She resorted to climbing in the back. I struggled to keep the grin off my face as Elayne leaned forward and told us what she'd learned that night.

16

SERENITY

I stared at my bacon cheeseburger, not feeling especially hungry. The day beyond the window was cloudy and threatening rain. The weather matched my mood perfectly.

"Do you want another sweet tea, darling?" Nancy's voice slashed into my depression.

I looked up at the diner's owner and my friend. She hadn't changed much since I'd worked part time at the diner as a teenager. She still had the same red hair, only now, it was from a box, and a sultry voice that most women only used in the bedroom.

"No, I'm good," I replied. Nancy gave Todd another cola and he thanked her. When she turned on her heel to leave, I found my voice again, "Nancy, have you had any experiences with spiritual healings?" I ventured, feeling stupid for asking.

Nancy's reaction caught me off guard. She flopped down in the seat, bumping into my side. "Funny you should ask. Just the other day, I was thinking about something I experienced a long time ago." She glanced around the diner, emptying from the noon rush, and lowered her voice. "When I was a little girl, my folks took me down to Tennessee to visit kin who lived there.

KAREN ANN HOPKINS

One Sunday morning, we ended up in a little cow-poke building in the middle of the woods. If I hadn't been told it was
a church, I never would have guessed it. It was nothing but a
square, wooden building sitting beneath a stand of pine trees.

"There was a mixture of whites and colored folk in the
congregation and they sang out loud as if the spirit was with
each and every one of them that day. Their hands were raised
to the ceiling, swaying back and forth. They even stomped
their feet. To be honest, their enthusiasm scared me. I remember clutching my momma's dress tightly in my hands as I hid
my face in the material."

Nancy paused and looked around again. Todd and I exchanged glances. His face was wide with curiosity as I'm sure
mine was.

When Nancy was satisfied there were no eavesdroppers,
she returned her attention to us and continued. "There was a
girl not much older than me at the service. She was slumped
in a wheelchair and her poor legs were skinny and unused.
Blonde hair hung in her face and she didn't even bother to
push it away. I watched as she was wheeled in front of the
pews. The singing stopped. That room had been dead silent,
everyone was holding their breath.

"A colored woman walked up to the girl. She was wearing
a long, rust-orange colored dress and her head was covered
with a folded piece of material that matched her dress. She
was tall, slender and old. When she had turned to the crowd,
her eyes were white. The woman was blind, but she moved
freely enough that you wouldn't notice her handicap until you
saw her ghost eyes.

"She placed one hand on the girl's legs and the other
on her head and she began chanting in a language I didn't

recognize. The congregation began singing. At first it was slow, soft and steady, then gradually rising to a chorus of loud shouts that equaled that of the old blind woman."

Nancy took a deep breath and swallowed. She tilted her head to look into my eyes. I noticed hers were moist with unfallen tears. "That air in that room became heavy, almost oppressive with all the emotion of the congregation—and with something else. I felt its presence and sealed my eyes closed. I was terrified to see whatever it was that had entered that room. The chanting of the old woman and the boisterous singing of the people had filled my ears, vibrating the pews and floor around me. After what seemed like an eternity and my body cramped with fatigue, the singing died down. Cheers erupted and my eyes popped open. That blonde girl was standing. She took four steps to fall into the waiting arms of her mother. She had been healed."

The three of us sat in silence. I wasn't sure what to say. Nancy's experience was different in some ways to what I'd witnessed with Mervin's healing, but there were enough similarities to make me squirm.

"Did you ever see anything like that again?"

"Nope, that was the only time," Nancy said, slapping her hand down on the table as she leaned back. "To this day, I don't know exactly what I saw."

I took a sip of my tea. "Are you aware the Amish call that sort of healing a laying of the hands? It's not very common, but it does happen in their communities."

"No kidding," Nancy exclaimed. "Does the entire congregation get involved?"

"I don't know for sure. But there's a shaman-type person who initiates the healing while the family members gather around and pray."

"It's kind of group hysteria if you ask me," Todd finally spoke up. When Nancy and I stared at him, he went on to say, "That girl you thought you saw healed might not have been really crippled. It could have been a sham set up to get more donations for a backwoods church." Todd's gaze rested on me. "Mervin Lapp's pain might have been his head. I asked Heather about it. She thought after this many months, he should have been feeling better anyway. The mind is an amazing thing. Sometimes sheer belief in something can make a person well. Look at all those people who beat cancer with a positive attitude. There've been studies about miracle healings and they usually come up with a scientific explanation."

"That still doesn't explain what I felt in that room. Maybe it was all in my mind, I don't know. But it sure felt real at the time," Nancy replied.

I touched her hand. "I believe you."

Nancy smiled back before she rose from the table and strutted to the counter.

"I didn't mean to piss her off," Todd muttered.

I rolled my eyes, about to respond when Bobby appeared at the end of the booth and took the seat Nancy had vacated. His brisk manner put me on high alert as he sifted through the files in his brief case. He pulled out a fax copy and handed it to me.

"That's the toxicology report on Fannie's tea cup," Bobby said.

I scanned the paper and looked back at the coroner. "Tansy ragwort and pennyroyal traces found in the cup, along with parsley, peppermint and lavender? What does this mean?"

"I've been online researching these herbs all morning. I even called a doctor friend of mine who practices internal medicine to verify my findings." Bobby paused to take a sip of the cola Nancy had brought him.

"What are you in the mood—?"

Bobby waved her away like a pesky fly. "Nothing right now."

Nancy snorted and left the table. I didn't comment.

Bobby turned back to me. "Both tansy and pennyroyal have medicinal properties, but can be dangerous if the dosage is off or the flowers themselves are highly potent. They're both abortifacients, used in the past to terminate unwanted pregnancy or regulate menstrual cycles. Combined, you have the makings for a lethal tea."

"What about the lavender and parsley?" I asked.

"The parsley is also used to bring on menses and has been labeled as a possible cause of miscarriage, but it's fairly benign as far as risk to the person taking it goes. Lavender has many uses, but one of those is a form of tranquilizer."

"What did your doctor friend think about the combination of ingredients?" I asked, already having a good idea what he was going to say.

"He basically said that no one in their right mind would mix those ingredients up and serve it to someone—unless they were trying to hurt them. Having both tansy and pennyroyal in the tea was complete overkill. The lavender probably made the girl too drowsy to even realize she was bleeding to death. The parsley is a bit of a curiosity, though."

"What are you putting down as cause of death?"

Bobby lifted his glasses from his nose and rubbed his eyes. "Did the girl know enough about herbs to make this concoction on her own?"

"No. From the sounds of it, she had no training or experience with herbs." I sighed. "But from what Elayne found out last night, she very well might have been attempting to end the pregnancy."

Bobby replaced his glasses and met my gaze. "What do you know?"

"Supposedly, neither the mother, nor the younger sister knew who the father was. Hannah did have an idea her sister was pregnant right before Fannie died. It sounds like she was in shock about it and was afraid to discuss the matter with anyone, including Fannie."

"Do you know who provided the tea for Fannie?" Bobby asked.

I shook my head. "Ada Mae Peachey confirmed that Jonas was treating Irene for her asthma and insomnia. She prepared the herbal treatments, but Jonas administered them. It's going to take some more digging to find out if he added an ingredient that made it a lethal herbal tea." I leaned back and glanced out the window as the first rain drops pelted the glass. "I still can't figure out why he'd want to kill Fannie in the first place. We're missing something."

"What about his wife—any information there that might help?"

I thought back to my encounter with Wilma Gingerich and her granddaughter, Marissa. Something wasn't sitting well with me about the visit, but there wasn't any one thing I could put my finger on.

"No, it seems like she bled out after delivering the baby. The hospital and death reports both listed it as natural causes stemming from childbirth."

"That's the interesting thing with this case," Bobby mused. "Women do occasionally die in pregnancy or during the course of delivery, even with our modern medical advancements.

Sometimes nature fails a woman and the cost is her life or her child's. It's often difficult to know exactly what happened, so they're lumped together in the *natural causes* basket. In actuality, something or someone could have contributed to the death and gotten away with it."

I became impatient. "Are you lumping Fannie's death into that same basket?"

Bobby met my hard gaze. "No. I believe the herbs she ingested sedated her and caused her to bleed out—contributing, if not causing, her death and that of the fetus. I'll mark the death as questionable suicide with ongoing investigation." He leaned closer. "We need to know where she got that drink from before I can upgrade it to a homicide. All those ingredients are common enough that even a simple woman could have mixed them together herself."

"I'll see what I can do. If you've done all the analysis you can on the body, go ahead and release her to the family."

Bobby nodded, stuffing his files back into the briefcase. "I heard you got shot at in the Amish settlement last night."

"Not exactly. I just happened to be in the Peachey household when their house got shot at."

"Hmm." He swirled the straw in his drink. "That's unexpected. I wonder what brought it on."

"We might get our answer right now," Todd said, lifting his chin toward the diner's entrance.

I looked over my shoulder at the four young men shaking off the rain from their jackets. With raised brows, I glanced back at Todd. "Are they our guys?"

"None other than." He smirked back at me.

Bobby slid from the booth. For an older guy, he sometimes surprised me with his spryness. "I'll leave you to it then. I've got to get back to the office. Ed is hounding me day and night to close the robbery file for the feds."

"Thanks, Bobby," I offered.

"Retirement is sounding better every day," Bobby mumbled as he left the table.

We waited until the four men were seated at a booth a couple down from us before we rose and joined them.

"I'm Sheriff Serenity Adams. I think you're all acquainted with Deputy Todd Roftin." I addressed the group, but took my time looking at each young man individually.

Two of the teens looked down at the table top and the other two met my gaze. None of them looked overly threatening, wearing jeans and t-shirts, a few tattoos visible, and some stubble. The scent of cigarette smoke clung to the one closest to me. The guy in the corner's nose was hooked and his dark hair fell over the side of his face like a pirate.

The pirate spoke for the group. "What can we do for you, Sheriff?" He swept his eyes over me.

I narrowed my eyes at him. "Are you Arlo Thomas?" I guessed.

"Sure am. Did I do something wrong?" He smirked, all mock innocence.

"Is that navy blue sedan parked in front of the restaurant yours?"

"Yeah. What of it?"

"It matches the description of a vehicle that forced a buggy off the road the other day. That wouldn't happen to be you, would it?" I kept my voice even, never taking my eyes from Arlo's face.

The guy who smelled like cigarette smoke began to stand, but Todd's hand on his shoulder shoved him back down. "You're not going anywhere just yet."

I glanced around. The few patrons scattered about the diner were pretending not to notice us, which was a good thing.

I rested my hands on the table and leaned forward, making eye contact with each man in turn, ending with Arlo.

"There will be no harassment of the Amish under my watch. I won't tolerate it. If you boys don't want to end up in the county jail, you'd best change your thinking and move on from any petty squabbles you may have with them." I dropped my voice.

The young man who had been trying to escape squeaked, "Yes, ma'am."

The other two nodded in unison, but not Arlo. He pushed the stray hairs from his face and stared back at me. His blatant disregard for authority didn't surprise me. There was one in every group. The deep emotions swirling around in the depths of his brown eyes got my attention. For this guy, it was personal.

"You can't keep me out of the settlement. I've got just as much right to be there as anyone else," he taunted.

"Not if you're breaking the law, you don't," I said.

Arlo chuckled. "You have no idea what's going on out there. Crazy shit that you wouldn't believe."

"Try me," I challenged.

Arlo took a deep breath and looked away. When he faced me, his face was set in stone and his eyes glinted.

"Whatever I've done was to protect my girl. No one else will," Arlo breathed.

I swallowed. "Who's your girl?"

"Hannah Kuhns."

17

SERENITY

Ten minutes later, Todd and I had Arlo Thomas inside the cruiser. Ethan, Davie, and Otis were waiting for his return in the diner.

"Am I under arrest?" Arlo asked from the backseat. He was still playing the tough guy, but I'd heard the crack in his voice. Arlo was off balance now, just the way I wanted.

"So tell me how you and Hannah Kuhns hooked up in the first place." I shifted in my seat to get a better view of Arlo's face.

"She was at the stockyard with some of the Amish girls the same day I met Eli." He shrugged and blushed at the same time. "I asked him to introduce us. He did and we sort of hit it off. She's a lot quieter than the girls I'm used to. With her daddy gone, she needed a man in her life, if you know what I mean."

The smirk returned and I wanted to smack his face. I took a deeper breath. "No, I don't know what you mean. Please explain."

Arlo met my gaze unflinchingly. "She wanted to fuck. I obliged her."

Todd made a growling noise and swiveled in the driver's seat. "Watch your mouth or I'll haul your ass into lockup for popping the Peachey house last night."

"What are talking about? I was at Charlie's Pub. There's at least a dozen people who saw me there," Arlo said.

I caught the surprised look on Arlo's face at Todd's accusation. He wasn't lying. Todd licked his lips, raising his brows at me.

I changed tactics. "Listen, Arlo, someone took a shot at the Peachy house last night. I was there and saw a sedan, similar to yours, speeding away. Given your involvement with Hannah and the bad blood between you and Eli, I have enough to take you in for formal questioning." I exhaled, putting on a show of hesitancy. "Or, if you have any information that might help us out, you can avoid that kind of trouble."

Arlo laughed and then sighed. "One of the Amish drivers drives a car like mine, only it's black. You might want to talk to her about it. That's all I got for you. If you're going to arrest me, then read me my rights. Otherwise, I'm out of here."

"We know where to find you," was all I said.

Todd got out of the cruiser and opened the door for Arlo. When Todd climbed back into the driver's seat, I watched Arlo saunter back into the diner like he didn't have a care in the world, even though the rain was pouring down onto his head.

The rain came down harder and a few seconds later, Todd had to turn up the wiper blades to see out the windshield at all.

"What a prick. A guy has to be a lowlife to go and do that to an Amish girl," Todd commented, not putting the car into gear yet.

"She's eighteen, old enough to decide who she wants to sleep with," I replied, too distracted to focus entirely on my partner. The streaks of water making paths down the glass darkened my mood.

"Hopefully, she can move on and forget about him. That would be the best thing for a girl like her. If the bishop finds out she was screwing around with an outsider like that, she'll be in a lot of trouble."

"She might already be in trouble." I glanced away, but not before I saw the look of shock cross over Todd's face.

"Oh, shit. That would be really bad," Todd commented.

"Maybe even more so than you can imagine." I met Todd's gaze. "You know what happened to her sister."

Todd put the car into gear. "Are we tracking down the Amish driver with the black sedan or visiting some other Amish folk?"

I was contemplating his question when Rosie's voice came over the radio asking for assistance with a vehicular accident on Route 48.

I smiled at Todd. "You take the wreck. My tires should be ready by now. If you don't mind dropping me off at my brother-in-law's repair shop, I'll be good to go."

Todd snorted. "You get to have all the fun."

The rain turned to drizzle and the sky opened up to reveal a rainbow in the distance.

Ironically, it appeared to be dropping from the sky right into the Amish settlement. I wasn't sure whether that was a good sign or not.

The roads were still slick when I entered the settlement, but faint sunshine sprinkled out through the clouds. A stiff breeze bent the trees down, indicating the rain would soon be returning.

Stuck behind a buggy going about five miles per hour, I backed off, not wanting to push the driver to work the brown, sweaty horse any harder than it already was.

As we rounded the bend, I noticed a crowd gathered at the end of Moses and Anna Bachman's driveway. A few were boys mounted on fidgeting horses, the rest were women and children. Their colorful dresses whipped around their legs in the wind, catching my eye. I recognized Anna, David's mother at once. The buggy pulled to a stop when it reached the crowd and was swamped by the onlookers.

I eased on the brakes, leaning out the window for a better look. Aaron Esch stepped out of the buggy, blocking the road. I pulled off into a little stretch of grass and cut my engine. I'd barely stepped out of the car when Anna spotted me. Her hand shot up and she hurried towards me, Aaron right behind her.

"Sheriff, we need your help," Anna called out.

I ran to them. We came together in the middle of the road.

"What's the emergency?" I pulled my cell phone from my pocket.

"It's my little granddaughter, Christina, and her friend, Lucy. They've been poisoned by cowbane," Anna reached out and grabbed my hand. You must take them to the hospital or they'll die."

I didn't even know what cowbane was, and the distance to the hospital was timely, even if I drove the children there myself. "Where are the girls?"

Anna pointed up the road. "At the next farm. Lucy's brother rode over to tell us. Aaron just happened to be passing by."

I looked up at the bishop and saw the hesitancy in his eyes. "The time it takes to get them to the hospital might be too much." He tugged on his long, white beard. "There is another option."

I held my breath, waiting for him to say it.

"I just left Jonas' place. He's there and so is Ada Mae. They might be able to help." The bishop's words lacked firmness.

"No, I don't want his hands on my granddaughter," Anna protested.

I looked back at the bishop and saw the intense conflict on his face. "It might be the only way to save them." He turned to me. "Go to the Peachey's, tell them that the girls were blowing whistles made from the hollow stems of water hemlock. They'll understand and know what to bring. Call your English ambulance on the way there. If the children survive, they'll need hospital care."

Aaron Esch was an intelligent man, I knew that. His commanding presence couldn't be taken lightly either. His plan was as sound as any that I could come up with.

I ran back to my car and shouted over my shoulder, "Clear the road, bishop. I don't want another tragedy on my hands."

As I made the U-turn, the bishop waved his hands, getting everyone away from the road. My heart pounded as I hit the gas pedal and dialed central dispatch.

Once again, a simple visit to the settlement to ask a few questions had turned into a race to save someone's life.

The thought trickled away when I pictured Daniel's little niece, Christina. I'd saved her life the previous fall when the child had slipped into a hole dug for a new ice house that had filled with rainwater. If I hadn't done CPR on her, she would have died.

Her life was once again in jeopardy. It made me question the workings of the universe.

I said a silent prayer for the girl as I pressed the gas pedal harder.

18

DANIEL

Ma's recorded message on my cellphone had been a jumbled mess of German and English. When I pulled in the Stolzfus' driveway, I wasn't sure what was going on other than that my niece and her friend had been poisoned. Luckily, I had been only a few miles away giving an estimate for new construction on a house when she'd called.

Seeing Serenity's car, along with several buggies, made my stomach clench. My girlfriend seemed to be a magnet for emergencies.

I squeezed through a small crowd of women and children waiting on the porch, slipping through the screen door without bothering to knock. The empty kitchen was dimly lit from the natural light of the rainy day outside.

I followed the sound of muted voices to the wooden staircase around the corner. Taking the steps two at a time, I made my way to the second floor. Holding my breath, I peeked into the room where the voices were coming from.

I made eye contact with Serenity. Her face was tight. My sister, Rebecca, was on one side of the bed, holding Christina upright in her lap. My niece was soaked in sweat and visibly shaking. Mrs. Stolzfus was beside Rebecca, holding her own little girl in her arms in the same manner. A quick glance showed her to be in the same state as Christina.

Ada Mae shook a glass bottle in her hand and poured its contents into two cups. Ma dropped a straw into each cup. She took one of them and thrusted it at Rebecca, who forced the straw into Christina's mouth. Ada Mae brought the other cup close to second girl's lips, mumbling encouraging words.

My heart raced as the scene unfolded. I was unable to do anything to help and that bothered me. Jonas raised his hand above his head and prayed out loud. The women in the room alternated from offering words of encouragement to praying. My gaze drifted back to Serenity.

She was staring at Christina, her mouth set in a grim line. When Jonas' voice grew louder, her eyes shifted to him.

There was a mesmerizing quality to the man's voice. He had evangelistic flare, a kind of charisma that most people weren't born with. He was confident in his words, like he believed someone was listening.

A gush of warm, stormy wind blew in from the opened window, but no one turned their heads to acknowledge it. The light rain tapped on the tin roof, giving the attempt to save the girls' lives a quieter, less urgent feel.

One of the words I had recognized over the phone call from Ma was *cowbane*, otherwise known as water hemlock. It was a highly poisonous weed that grew freely in many pastures in the area. Oftentimes, livestock were poisoned by ingesting the plants. Depending on the part of the plant and how much they ate, they'd show signs of poisoning within minutes.

Abdominal pain, tremors and seizures soon followed. Usually the animal died.

When I was growing up, a boy in the community had taken a bite out of the root of the plant on a dare. The roots held the most poison. The boy died a few hours later. Even the doctors in the hospital couldn't save him.

The Stolzfus girl was the first to begin coughing. Ada Mae was ready with a towel to catch the girl's vomit when she began throwing up. Her mother cried and thanked God. The child wasn't out of the woods, but throwing up some of the poison would help.

Serenity's hand curled around mine when I reached her side, and looked down at her. She forced a smile and rubbed my hand. I put my arm around her shoulders and squeezed. Our gazes returned to little Christina.

Ma sat on the edge of the bed, her eyes closed and her mouth working in silent prayer. Rebecca continued to urge Christina to drink the dark liquid.

Sirens blared in the distance and Serenity looked up. She let go of my hand and disappeared through the doorway. Her footsteps pounded down the staircase.

Even though I barely knew my niece, my heart clenched at the sight of her possibly dying right in front of me. The combination of my sister's and mother's grief wafted around them, like a punch of solidness in the air.

Christina shook, bouncing in her mother's arms. Jonas prayed louder, asking the Lord to leave the girl with her family, but allowing that if Christina was to be at his side this day, that her delivery be painless and brief.

The words echoed in my mind. What if it were my child lying there? Could I so easily give her up if that's what God intended?

The coughing fit that followed Christina's shaking caused her to throw up into Ma's apron. The smile that spread onto Ma's face showed her pleasure that the drink had worked.

Serenity burst into the room with the two paramedics I'd seen at the Kuhns' farm days earlier.

Ada Mae spoke up, directing her words to the female paramedic. "We gave the girls activated charcoal. They both threw up. It's water hemlock poisoning. Seems they were using the stems as blowing whistles."

The paramedics went to work, splitting up to check the vital signs of each girl. "How long ago did they have the plant in their mouths?" the man asked as he checked Christina's pupils with a small flashlight.

"It's been about fifteen minutes since the girls came in complaining of belly aches. They were drooling, too. That's when I asked what they got into," Mrs. Stoltzfus answered.

"Raymond, how bad is it?" Serenity asked.

Raymond exhaled, glancing from Serenity to Ada Mae. "It looks like these folks have saved the little girls with their quick thinking. We would have administered the charcoal at the hospital, but it might have been too late." His gaze fell on Ada Mae. "Good job."

She nodded curtly. Before she turned away, her face flushed.

The paramedics, with the help of the Amish women, loaded the girls into the ambulance with their mothers. I watched the vehicle carefully maneuver around the fidgeting horses, waiting until it reached the roadway before blaring their sirens. I figured the local authorities were used to dealing with emergency situations arising in the Amish settlement. From what I'd witnessed, they were doing a fine job adjusting to the cultural differences.

"That was insane," Serenity mumbled. She'd walked up quietly behind me to stand at the porch railing.

I placed my hand over hers. "Never a dull moment."

Jonas and Ada Mae came through the front door together. Standing side-by-side, I saw the sibling resemblance. They were both tall, proud people. Looking at them now, I had a difficult time feeling anything except respect for them. Their knowledge and ways had saved my niece and another child.

"Thank you for what you did in there," I said, extending my hand to Jonas. He grasped it quickly, with a small smile.

"It's what we were born to do. The Lord gave us the ability to heal. We are under his guidance always."

I didn't bother to reach for Ada Mae's hand. I knew the Amish ways. She'd be uncomfortable with such contact. I met her gaze and nodded my thanks. She smiled back weakly and glanced away.

"Mr. Peachey, do you have a few minutes to answer some more questions about the Kuhns' case?" Serenity asked.

I glanced at her, thinking it wasn't the right time for another interrogation.

"Sure." Jonas looked at Ada Mae, who shrugged back at him. "We can spare that much time, I think."

We waited for the crowd to disperse as we stood beside Jonas' horse and buggy. Verna had driven the buggy to the Stolzfus' farm after her father and aunt had been spirited away by Serenity in her car. The Amish girl stood a little ways down the hill, talking to Mervin. He had been one of the boys who'd ridden throughout the neighborhood spreading news of the girls' poisoning. His limp was gone and something about his straight-backed posture made me confident that the injuries to his heart from Naomi's death were healing, too.

I smiled. It was amazing what a girl could do for a boy.

Serenity saw the look on my face and raised her brows. I lifted my chin and her gaze followed the direction to the love-struck teens. Now that the emergency had passed and the stormy skies were lifting, exposing shards of bright sunlight, I felt hopeful again. Serenity and I would be all right.

The area around the buggy fell quiet, and Serenity pulled out her notebook from her pocket. She flipped through the pages, reading briefly to herself. She looked at Jonas.

"Mr. Peachey, do you have tansy ragwort and pennyroyal among the herbs you keep?" Serenity asked.

Jonas turned to Ada Mae, who answered the question. "Yes, we keep all kinds of herbs in supply." She pointed back to the Stoltzfus house. "You never know what you're going to face on any given day. Those girls would be dying, beyond help right now, if I had to take the time to search out the ingredients needed to force them to regurgitate the plant."

It made sense. I glanced at Serenity, anxious at her narrowed gaze.

"What do you personally use those two herbs for?" Serenity continued.

Ada Mae didn't hesitate. "The tansy I give for worms. Sometimes I make a concoction to keep the insects away. Pennyroyal helps keep a woman's bleeding regular and less painful. It soothes PMS symptoms," she said.

Serenity took a deep breath. Her gaze swept between Jonas and Ada Mae, but landed squarely on the woman when she said, "Do you have any idea why those two ingredients would be mixed together and drank as a tea?"

Ada Mae's eyes widened. "Why, no one in their right mind would drink those two together. They are tricky on their own. Combined, they might be very dangerous indeed."

"Were either of you aware that Fannie was five months pregnant?" Serenity plowed on.

Jonas reddened with embarrassment, glancing away. He mumbled. "No. That's not something I knew of."

Ada Mae frowned. The expression made me stare harder at her.

"I suspected she was," Ada Mae admitted. "For my people, it's not expected that an unmarried woman will be pregnant. She complained of belly aches in the morning and I gave her peppermint tea to calm her stomach." Ada Mae shifted on her feet, taking a sharp breath. "She told me that her menses were off and asked what herbal remedy might help. I told her to try a small amount of parsley in her tea."

Serenity digested Ada Mae's words and then shut her notebook. "We're still working on the person who shot out your window. We have an idea who it might be, but don't have anything definitive. If you see any cars, especially dark colored, four door types parking near your farm, please call me immediately." Serenity handed Ada Mae a business card.

Ada Mae flicked her hand over her shoulder. "Like that one?"

"Yeah, exactly," Serenity said smoothly. She tipped her hat at Jonas and Ada Mae before nodding her head for me to follow her down the driveway.

When we got close enough to see inside the black, four door sedan, my chest tightened.

Eli Bender sat in the front passenger seat.

19

SERENITY

Seriously? Eli Bender's lips were pinched and a wavy fold of thick, brown hair dropped down from his straw hat to almost cover one of his eyes. He was a good looking young man and the arrogant lift of his chin told me he knew it. It was the same attitude that had made me suspicious that he'd been the one who shot Naomi. She'd been pregnant with his child at the time. Combine that with the teen's defensive posture and he'd been a main suspect.

When I leaned into the vehicle, I studied the driver as well. I guessed her to be in her thirties. She was a heavy-set woman with short cropped, blond hair and thin lips. I couldn't see her eyes from the wide brimmed sunglasses she wore, but she smiled at me.

"Hi there, Sheriff. Are the girls going to be okay?" the woman asked in an overly familiar fashion.

Her outgoing manner bugged me. She was trying too hard.

"They're on their way to Blood Rock Regional Hospital," I said. "What's your name?"

"Jenny Reynolds. I drive the Amish to make some extra cash," she answered.

I tilted my head to look at Eli. He pushed the hair from his brow and stared back.

"And what are you two up to?" I directed the question at Eli, but Jenny answered.

"I was taking Eli to the crew he works with when we passed by some neighbors on the road. They told us what happened and I thought we'd stop in to see if there was anything we could do to help. Now that we know they're already on their way to the hospital, there's no need for us to intrude." Jenny smiled brightly, shifting the car's gear stick.

Her sudden desire to be away made me raise my hand. "Hold on a minute." I gazed at Eli. "I didn't get to talk to you the other night. I have a question for you."

Eli snorted.

"Do you know Hannah Kuhns?" Eli's body stiffened. It was as if I'd brought up Naomi.

He recovered quickly. "Of course I do. She lives in our community. We all know each other to some extent."

"She's the same age as you, isn't she?" I didn't miss a beat.

"I think so. What does it matter?" Eli asked, his lips twisting. His blue eyes squinted into the sun light.

The kid still had one hell of a chip on his shoulder.

I leaned in further. Eli held his ground. I dropped my voice and ignored Jenny's gaping mouth. "I'm only going to ask you this one time, Eli. I really hope that you learned from Naomi's case how important it is to be fully honest with the authorities." He lifted his eyes, waiting. "Are you courting, hoping to court or involved with Hannah Kuhns in any way, shape or form?"

Eli's shoulders slumped and his mouth opened. My breathing slowed with anticipation.

Just as Eli was about to speak, Jenny out maneuvered him. "Is this formal questioning, Sheriff? Because it doesn't seem proper if it is."

My gaze shot to Jenny. I removed my sunglasses, narrowing my eyes at her. I took a measured breath, reining in the explosion of anger at the sight of the woman's feigned ignorance.

"It was simply a question. And if Eli answers it honestly, there won't be any need for anything more formal," I said, returning my gaze to Eli.

"Nope. She's just another girl around here," Eli said, staring straight ahead.

I noticed the lift at the side of Jenny's mouth.

Pulling my notebook out, I walked to the back of the car and wrote the license plate number down.

"Hey, what are you doing?" Jenny called, leaning out the window.

"You have a tail light out. I'm mailing you a citation when I get back to my office. Be on the lookout for it."

"You can't do that!" Jenny shouted.

"Actually, I can." I flipped the notebook shut.

Jenny's mouth rounded into an O, but she didn't say anything else. Eli didn't make eye contact with me as the car backed up and rolled back down the driveway.

Falling into line right behind the car was the Peachey's buggy. Verna's hand shot out the small, square window at Mervin. He waved back, smiling.

A moment later, Mervin was trotting down the driveway on his horse.

I rested my hands on my hips, staring at the various modes of transportation departing from the Stoltzfus' farm. This was one of those times when I actually stopped to think how odd it was.

"What's going on in your head?" Daniel's voice cut though my thoughts.

"Eli just lied to me. I'd bet money that he has something going on with Hannah Kuhns and that's why he had a falling out with Arlo Thomas. Only a girl makes young men act so unreasonable," I said, sighing.

"What does it matter who he's sweet on? I don't see the connection," Daniel said.

I glanced up at his tall frame. He was frowning, which wasn't unusual, but the set of his jaw and the tightness around his eyes told me that he had things other than Eli Bender on his mind. I looked away. I was the reason he was so stressed. I should have bought the damn test and gotten it over with. I owed it to the man to at least give him an answer. He'd always been good to me. More than good, actually.

But this wasn't the time to get into that. I flushed the line of thought away and listened to the retreating *clip clops* of the horse on the pavement. I couldn't say much about Hannah. Seeing her buy a pregnancy test seemed too personal to mention. Even if it wasn't, I wasn't sure if it played into Fannie's situation. Either way, it made me extremely uncomfortable that two young women in the same Amish household became pregnant without a marriage or official courtship. The odds were stacked heavily against something like that. I'd learned a long time ago that when things appeared off, they usually were.

"I have my reasons," I said. "Have you already made plans with Elayne for dinner tonight?"

Daniel growled. "That's not fair. I spent time with her last night to help you with the investigation. That's it." He looked at me sternly. "Don't make something out of nothing." He took a breath and when he continued, his tone was softer. "I was hoping you'd join me. I'd be happy to grill steaks at the house or we could check out the new Italian restaurant on Main Street. It's your choice."

I fought the smile that threatened to erupt on my lips. To have a quiet evening was a novelty. Fannie's pale form lying on the examining table flashed before my eyes. I still didn't want to let it go. I might never be able to figure out what happened to Jonas' wife, Robyn, but Fannie's death was fresh enough that I could discover the truth.

Jonas was creepy, but he'd proven to be helpful in a strange, supernatural kind of way. Ada Mae was one of the few Amish women I'd met who was confident enough to take action into her own hands to save lives. They'd saved a couple of girls, making them valuable members of this community.

Maybe Fannie had tried to abort her own pregnancy by mixing ingredients together, not fully understanding the risks. I rubbed the side of my temple, pushing at the throbbing that was beginning to grow.

"Let's just eat in. I'm not in the mood for being out in public tonight."

"Sounds wonderful." Daniel smiled, taking my hand as he walked me to my car.

"Wait!" I looked over my shoulder. Anna Bachman scuttled down the hill towards us. We stopped and waited for her.

"I'll give you a ride to the hospital if you want," Daniel offered his mother.

"Oh, that would be very welcome," she said. The apron she'd been wearing that her granddaughter had thrown up in was gone. "I wanted to get cleaned up," she said.

Daniel bent down and kissed me on the lips in front of his mother. I stood stiffly beneath him at the abrupt action. Anna's eyes widened, but she didn't comment.

"What time are you coming over?" Daniel asked.

"It won't be too long. I have some matters to wrap up at the office," I said.

Anna spoke up. "Once again, I find myself in your debt, Sheriff." I shook my head, beginning to interrupt her when she stopped me with a raised hand. "If you hadn't gone to get Jonas and Ada Mae, bringing them back so quickly, those precious children would be with the Lord."

I swallowed and glanced away, heat warming my cheeks. Bishop Esch stood quietly to the side. Our eyes met. I got the feeling he wanted to talk to me.

"I'm just glad I was here to help," I told Anna.

"You look a little tired yourself. Try to get some rest," Anna said, before she turned away heading towards Daniel's Jeep. He smiled at me and joined his mother.

When I was alone with the bishop, he said, "What are your thoughts?"

I looked at the older man, more confused than ever.

"Fannie's death wasn't completely natural. The official report won't be out for a few days, but it's safe to say that she ingested a combination of ingredients that either caused her to bleed to death or exacerbated the event."

"What about Wilma Gingerich? Did she have anything new to add regarding my sister's death?" He asked the question slowly.

The breeze warmed as more of the clouds pushed to the east. I held my face into the soft wind and recalled my visit with Wilma. Even with the rise in temperature, I shivered.

"Nothing that can be used to indicate foul play. I looked over Robyn's medical records from when she was admitted to the hospital and the autopsy report. Everything points to natural death from childbirth complications."

The bishop nodded. He shifted on his feet to leave when he paused. His expression was guarded, thoughtful even. "I consider myself to be an honest and open minded man. I try to see the good in people, over the bad, always hoping that others are living same God fearing life that I am. I must admit, my sister's death has hounded me for a decade. I can't put my finger on it, something is not right to me." He shrugged. "Perhaps it's because Jonas' own mother perished in childbirth when Jonas and Ada Mae were teenagers."

"Did both the mother and baby die?"

"Yes, it was Violet Peachey's ninth child. The pregnancy was hard on her. It was a high risk for a woman of her age and fragile state to have another. A mistake that they all regretted later on," Bishop Esch said.

"Did she die in the home?" I asked, holding my breath.

"Why yes. It was Jonas and Ada Mae who cared for her. Their skills weren't enough to save their own mother."

"That is odd," I muttered.

"Yes, it is," the bishop said. He stared at me and then walked away.

I felt the thrumming of my heart as I imagined Jonas seeing both his mother and wife die in the birthing bed.

What were the chances of them both being natural deaths? I didn't like the direction my mind was going.

I glanced at the sun's low position in the western sky and made a quick decision.

I wouldn't be able to enjoy the evening with Daniel or work up the nerve to go back to the drug store to buy a pregnancy test until I visited one more person today.

I only hoped she'd talk to me.

20

SERENITY

I brought the tea cup to my mouth pretending to sip it. When I glanced over the rim, Hannah was fidgeting with her fingers in her lap, not touching her own cup.

Damn, I'm getting way too paranoid. I set my cup on the small table beside my chair. For once, I'd gotten a break. Irene Kuhns was in town, signing the release papers for Fannie's body. The burial was planned for the following afternoon. The Amish didn't waste time getting their dead into the ground.

"I'm sorry to ask you questions during such a difficult time." I searched Hannah's face, which was pale and tired. "Were you and Fannie close?"

Hannah sniffed, looking away. When she faced me again, her eyes had a slightly hard edge that took me by surprise. "This probably sounds awful, but no. We weren't close at all. She always bossed me around, making me do her chores. She was kind of lazy that way." Hannah blew out a long breath. "I feel terrible even thinking ill thoughts about her now after what's happened."

I studied Hannah's face. She was prettier than her sister. Her hair had a reddish tint and her large, hazel eyes were speckled with brown dots. Her nose was small and straight and her cheekbones high enough to be slightly exotic for an Amish girl. I could see Arlo Thomas going after her, and Eli Bender, too.

"It's not your fault. Sometimes, siblings don't get along. It happens." I tapped my finger on the table, debating how to proceed. She was eighteen, not a girl, but without any makeup and with the primly white cap, she seemed younger. "When did you find out about your sister's pregnancy?"

Hannah swallowed and her face reddened, but she didn't look away. "She'd been throwing up in the mornings and her belly was growing plumper. She never told me, but I suspected. Then when she began drinking the peppermint tea that Ada Mae brought her, I knew it for sure." She tilted her head, smirking, showing me how clever she thought she was. "All the pregnant women drink it to soothe their bellies."

"Did you notice your sister drinking any other kind of tea—perhaps something Jonas brought her?" I chanced.

Hannah scrunched up her mouth. "None that I can recall. Mr. Peachey stopped by with herbs for Momma each week. He would talk to Fannie, show attention to her." Hannah rolled her eyes. "That made Fannie's head get all big."

"Oh, really—why's that?"

Hannah shrugged. "Jonas Peachey is old, but he's a good looking man. He's still of marrying age." She glanced around, wide-eyed. Even though we were alone in the nearly dark house, she still feared being overheard. Only one lantern light glowed from above the kitchen table in the adjoining room.

The darkness made me uncomfortable, but didn't seem to bother Hannah. "I think Fannie was a little sweet on him."

Interesting. I filed the information away.

"Was your sister secretly seeing someone?" I lifted my shoulders apologetically. "I mean, we all know she was pregnant."

Hannah's face scrunched as if pained. From experience, I didn't think she was attempting to come up with a lie. The young woman seemed honest to a fault.

"I wondered that myself, but she never told me if she was seeing someone." She shrugged. "It's not unusual for secret courtships to go on. It's hard for us. Once we commit to courting, it's kind of a done deal. Sometimes teens will explore their possibilities in secret before announcing a firm courtship. It can save a lot of trouble later on."

I nodded slowly, understanding.

"What about you? Has someone caught your eye?" I ventured.

Hannah smiled, blushed, and then frowned. The passing of emotions over her face was startling to witness.

Her voice lowered to a whisper. "There's a boy I fancy a lot. But I think I messed it up."

A lump formed in my throat and my heart went out to the young woman sitting in front of me.

"Nothing is ever as bad as it seems," I offered.

"Oh, this is. I've ruined my life." Her eyes teared up. She pulled her apron up to dab at them.

I could feel her desperation. I reached over and grasped her hand. "Don't say that. There's always hope."

Hannah's wet eyes met mine and her tears began to fall. She stood up, jerking her hand away.

"All my hope is gone!" she cried, fleeing the room, her footsteps striking the wooden steps of the staircase.

I leaned back, exhaling.

Counseling wasn't my strong suit, but the girl needed help. I was going to get it for her before some kind of harm befell her, either from outside forces or from herself. The problem was, how to go about it? She was Amish. There was almost no way to get her the help she needed without the entire community finding out—including Eli.

I ran my hand through my hair, tugging on my ponytail. What a rotten turn of events for Hannah.

I would tell Daniel about the pregnancy test I'd seen Hannah buy and about what Arlo Thomas had said about the Amish girl. They were his people. He'd know how to handle it.

I stood and stretched, anxious to get out of the lonely, dark house.

When my cell phone vibrated in my pocket, I pulled it out, looking at the number.

Black Willow, Ohio. With my heart racing, I brought the phone to ear.

"Hello?"

"*Hullo?*"

"Who's this?" I asked.

"It's Marissa. Can you come talk to me?"

A picture of the mentally handicapped Amish girl came to mind. I'd given my business card to Wilma. Marissa must have gotten a hold of it.

"Uh, sure, but you're in another state. Why don't you tell me what's on your mind? We can talk on the phone," I suggested.

There was static and then a loud sigh. "I don't know. I'm not sure that's a good idea. I have something to tell you—to tell you about Jonas," Marissa sang into the phone.

"Okay, I'll come to you. Can you tell me what it's about?"

"Tell you about Jonas…tell you about Jonas…about Jonas." Marissa's singing stopped and the phone went dead.

I groaned, sprinting for the doorway.

So much for a relaxing evening.

21

SERENITY

I gazed out the window at the flat farmland softly illuminated by the full moon. Occasionally, a farmhouse and barns would appear, shadowed and eerie looking. Statistics showed more crimes were committed in urban areas, but there was something secretive about the lonely countryside that put me on edge more than the city centers I'd worked in. At least in Indianapolis, I knew what I was dealing with. Out here, I was constantly being surprised.

"I still don't see why we couldn't have left in the morning," Daniel remarked.

I took another sip of the milkshake he'd bought me at the last rest stop. It was chocolate-banana, my favorite. Glancing over at his profile, I smiled. He really was accommodating.

"If you had heard Marissa on the phone, you'd be in a hurry to get there too," I pointed out.

Daniel ran his hand through his hair. "If she's not in any danger, I don't agree. She's a simpleton. You can't trust what she says to be factual anyway."

I shook my head. "I disagree. Marissa is functional. She might be at the intellectual level of a child, but she's capable of explaining herself." I took a shuttering breath. "She has a secret about Jonas and I want to know what it is."

"Even if she does, will her testimony be admissible in court?"

I took a measured breath. "It's hard to say. I'm hoping that whatever she has to say opens up new channels to investigate Jonas Peachy. Marissa might just have enough information to break the case wide open, without having to involve her too much in the details."

Daniel's voice dropped. "Why is it so important for you to nail this guy to the wall? Has it ever occurred to you that maybe he's innocent? We don't even know for sure what happened to Fannie."

I stared at Daniel, taking in his strong nose and full lips. Whenever I stared too long, I experienced school-girl tingles, and this time was no different. I shook off the feeling.

"There's something up with him. I can't put my finger on it, but my gut is telling me that he's crooked." I turned in the seat to face Daniel. "Do the Amish commit suicide? I remember Rachel Yoder stepped in front of a train because of her feelings of guilt about Tony Manning's beating, but does that sort of thing happen often?"

Daniel shook his head. "No. They believe suicide is the ultimate sin. The Lord will forgive for grievous acts, but once you've killed yourself, you can't ask forgiveness. Honestly, Rachel Yoder is the only person I know of who did themselves in intentionally."

"That's what makes Fannie's case so strange," I exclaimed. "The herbs she ingested either killed her outright or worsened a situation arising from complications of the pregnancy. Either way, she consumed ingredients that were highly dangerous. Even if she was desperate, it seems an odd way for a young woman to take her life."

"Who's to say? Maybe she simply mixed some herbs together in the hopes of having an abortion and it killed her too," Daniel suggested.

"I checked with Bobby on this. Tansy ragwort and pennyroyal aren't the types of herbs that common people have laying around in their kitchens."

"We're talking about the Amish, remember. There are many uses for herbs. I distinctly remember Ma having a variety of dried plants hanging from the rafters in the storeroom when I was growing up. You've seen firsthand how important herbal remedies are to the Plain people. Look how Ada Mae was able to save Christina and her friend."

I sank down into the seat, thinking. It wasn't just plants on my mind.

"What about the supernatural healings? Do you really believe that your friend Lester was miraculously healed by your mother or that Mervin's leg recovered because of some kind of Amish magic?"

Daniel was silent a moment, then chuckled. "Why is it so difficult for you to believe in things you can't see? That's what faith is, Serenity. Trusting in something because you feel it on the inside, not because you see it in front of your face."

I rolled my eyes, but didn't immediately say anything. I had seen Mervin's healing. It was the spooky feeling that rolled over me when Jonas had been praying that was my undoing.

"I can't deny that *something* happened in that room with Mervin. That's what scares me," I admitted.

Daniel reached over and cupped my hand. He smiled. "The sooner you accept that not everything is explainable, the happier you'll be."

I took a breath. "This case is different than others I've worked on, especially Naomi's. Usually, I have a clear idea about what's going on. This time I don't. It's as if the entire case is fogged over."

Daniel released my hand and turned into Wilma Gingerich's driveway. It was still the same little white house beside the road, surrounded by yellow flowers, but in the shadows of night, it wasn't as welcoming.

Daniel cut the engine off and turned to me. "It's almost nine o'clock. That's really too late to call on Wilma uninvited."

"I know." I sighed. "But I have no choice. That girl needs my help. That's one thing I am sure of," I said.

Without argument, Daniel stepped out of the Jeep. I followed suit. I found myself standing on the front porch with my arms crossed. The nighttime air was chilly and still.

Daniel rapped on the door. Only a faint light shone from a window on the side of the house. I waited, holding my breath that we hadn't wasted a three hour drive.

The door opened a crack and Wilma peeked out. She wasn't wearing the usual cap. Her long gray hair was coiled onto her head. The wrinkles in her face deepened when she saw me.

"*Warum sind sie heir?*"

Daniel answered her in English. "I'm sorry. Your granddaughter, Marissa, called Serenity on the phone earlier. She said that it was an urgent matter that she talk to her."

Wilma snorted, straightening her bent body to address me. "Marissa's mind does not work properly. Didn't you see that for yourself?"

I took a step forward. "She can still see things—understand them. The case I'm working back in Blood Rock is serious. A young woman died. I want to make sure there was no foul play involved before I close the case."

Wilma's mouth tightened, but she cracked the door open a little further. "I'll see if she's still awake. She has trouble falling asleep most nights. That girl is plagued with nightmares. Her soul is restless."

Wilma shuffled away. I finally breathed. Daniel and I exchanged glances, but neither of us spoke.

A moment later, Wilma was back at the door, a frown curving her thin lips.

"She's not in her bed," she said.

My heart began pounding. "Where could she be?"

Wilma shrugged. "*Ach*, that girl. Sometimes when she can't sleep, she wanders down to the pond behind the house. Check there first."

Wilma's voice was thick with annoyance. Marissa's disappearance didn't seem to worry her.

I felt the press of urgency to get to the pond. Leaving Wilma at the door, I jogged down the porch steps. Daniel was right behind me.

We didn't slow from a run until we reached the pond that dropped away from a steep bank on the near side. Slowing, to pick my way more carefully, I stepped through the taller grass, searching for Marissa with wide eyes. The pond was more like a small lake. The far side was mowed right up to the water's edge, but on either side were bushes and brush trees crowding together. The scent of scum and mud reached my nostrils and the sound of hundreds of chirping frogs filled my ears.

"There," Daniel said, pointing across the water to a place along the shore where a tree had fallen.

Marissa's light colored dress stuck out like a beacon in the moonlight.

I titled my head to listen. Marissa's quiet singing carried over the water.

"I have something to tell you—to tell you about Jonas. Tell you about Jonas...tell you about Jonas....about Jonas."

I shivered and walked faster.

When I reached the Amish woman, her singing stopped. She smiled at me.

I bent to my knees in front of her. Daniel hung back, crossing his hands over his chest.

"Marissa, I'm here. You can tell me what you wanted to about Jonas," I urged.

Marissa looked over my shoulder and then at Daniel, searchingly. "Is Jonas with you?" she inquired.

I shook my head. "No. He's back in Blood Rock. He lives there now, but he used to live here, didn't he?"

Marissa's smile deepened. "Yes, he did. He would visit me, here at the pond on nice evenings like this."

The erratic beating of my heart continued as suspicions formed.

"Would Jonas come here alone?" I motioned to the lonely country scene around the pond. Mist rose from the water, adding to the horror movie feel of the place.

She nodded, then frowned. "But he doesn't come no more—no more."

I glanced at Daniel. His eyes were wide with apprehension. I felt the same way. Some things you needed to know, but didn't really want to.

I took a steadying breath. "What did you and Jonas do when he came to see you?"

Even in the dull light from the moon, I saw Marissa blush. She began humming the same tune.

I listened to the soulful sound, staring out at the water, my mind wandering to another time when Jonas Peachey was here with Marissa, alone.

"And then came the bleeding—the bleeding—the bleeding." In jarring fashion, Marissa began singing.

I touched her shoulder lightly and she jumped. She turned to face me. Her eyes were clear.

"Why did you bleed?" I coaxed.

"It hurt." She gripped her stomach as if feeling the pains again. "It hurt down my belly and my back and my legs, and then came the blood." She dropped her voice, leaning in. "I thought I was dying. All that blood and the stuff too. It all came out."

I tried to wrap my mind around what she was saying. I felt dirty just thinking about it.

"Do you know why you bled like that?" I asked.

"The baby came out," she whispered and pointed at the stand of trees. "He's over there. I put him in the ground, like I do the dead chickens."

My eyes drifted to the shadowy place under the trees. I swallowed. "Did Jonas come to you after that happened?"

Marissa shook her head. "Jonas went away—went away."

The sadness in her voice pulsated. I exhaled slowly, trying to steady the pounding anger that grew inside of me.

I stood up, taking Marissa's hand into my own. "Your grandmother is waiting for you back at the house. Go on."

Marissa's expression changed to happiness once again. "Going to the house—I'm going to the house—going to the house," she sang. Her steps were light and quick as she made her way back around the pond.

She seemed to have forgotten Jonas and everything else. For Marissa, ignorance really was bliss. It was probably for the best.

When the flash of Marissa's dress disappeared around the corner of the house, I turned back to Daniel.

"I didn't see that coming," Daniel said, rubbing his face.

I lifted my chin and stepped under the branches of the trees.

"No—you're not serious." Daniel caught up to me and grasped my arm.

I looked up at him. "Because of Marissa's state of mind, her statements won't be taken seriously by a judge. We need proof that she's telling the truth." I clucked under my breath. "Are you going to help me or is this too much for you to handle?"

Daniel half rolled his eyes and sighed. "This is a little above and beyond the call of duty for the average boyfriend," Daniel quipped, but he stepped in front of me, taking the lead.

"Is that what you are—an average boyfriend?" I said.

Daniel stopped, turning abruptly.

He pulled me into his arms and brought his mouth down hard on mine. I was too surprised to pull back. After Marissa's jumbled story, Hannah's desperate situation and visions of Fannie's pale, dead form, Daniel's kiss blotted out the icky feeling that had taken hold of me.

Daniel's tongue explored my mouth as his hands rubbed up and down my back. I melted into his chest. For a brief time, I forgot about the Amish women and their pregnancies, but as Daniel's hands became bolder, cupping my breast, thoughts of Jonas doing the same thing to Marissa invaded my thoughts.

She was a woman on the outside, but mentally, only a child. For her to have a miscarriage, barely even understanding what had happened to her was beyond awful. My stomach rolled and I pulled away, staring back at him.

At first he frowned, then the look shifted to resolve.

"Let's get this over with," he said, turning back to his original course.

He stopped at a small pile of rocks and I stared down at them. They were too orderly to be the random placement of nature.

I rolled up my sleeves. *This is the part of the job that really sucked.*

22

SERENITY

"I made a call to the local sheriff in Ohio. He's aware of the situation," I said, handing the box to Bobby.

Bobby shook his head. "You don't want to bypass protocol, Serenity. If it comes to a court case, the way you handled that simple woman." He held up the box. "And this could mean the difference of a conviction or acquittal."

I flopped down in the chair, spreading my arms wide. "I know. When can you let me know for sure that it's human remains?"

"Give me an hour with it." Bobby dipped his head to peek over his glasses. "If it turns out to be a fetus, where are you heading with the investigation?"

I gazed out the window in my office. A stiff breeze was bending the tree branches along Main Street. The sun was bright, but the skies were full of dark clouds to the west. The feeling of foreboding was heavy and dark, and grim thoughts occupied my mind. The skeletal remains in the box were only a few inches long with a small amount of dried tissue clinging to the bones. The dirt and decomposition made it difficult to judge what it belonged to at a glance. If it wasn't for Marissa's story and her direction to the grave, I would have thought the remains were of a small woodland animal.

"If that's a fetus, I'm going to nail Jonas Peachey to a wall."

Bobby made a huffing noise and took the seat across the desk from me.

"Procreating isn't a crime," he said.

I leaned over the desk, crossing my arms beneath me. "Are you kidding me? Marissa has a child's mind. What Jonas Peachey did to her was wrong on every level."

Bobby nodded. "Let me play devil's advocate here. Marissa might be mentally challenged, but she is still an adult. She's living in a woman's body and she's allowed the same freedoms with that body that everyone else has."

"He's Amish." My voice rose. "He shouldn't have been bothering her in the first place."

He held up his hands. "I'm not disagreeing with you—just trying to get you to see the entire picture, all the angles. When you can wrap your mind around the entire scene, you'll see so much more."

I stood up and paced the room. "If those are the remains of a fetus, I'm arresting Jonas Peachey for Fannie's murder. There might be enough circumstantial evidence to make a case if it looks like he left Black Willow at about the same time Marissa miscarried. The timing of his departure could be coincidence, but I don't think it is. He was running away from a problem—one that his community there wouldn't tolerate." A picture of Hannah popped into my mind. "I'm afraid that as long as he's free, another girl might be in danger."

Bobby rose from his chair. "Give me an hour."

I was just about to follow Bobby out the door, when Todd came in.

"I thought you'd want to go on this call with me," he said, smirking.

I rolled my eyes. "I'm waiting on something important from Bobby. I think I should stick close to office."

"Even if the call involves Arlo Thomas and Eli Bender?"

I paused. "Okay. I'm listening."

Eli leaned up against the cattle pen, staring at the bull. His lips twisted stubbornly. The black and purple bruising on the side of his face was darkening. Several drops of blood marred his ivory, button-up shirt. His suspenders were pulled down over his shoulders, resting on his hips.

I glanced across the pens at Todd, who was talking to Arlo. Ethan Rent, Davie Chambers and Otis Green were standing a few away.

"Four to one. Not very good odds, if you ask me," I commented.

Eli looked up. Even with his battered face, the kid was still good looking. His lips rose in a wary smile. "I held my own just fine," he snapped.

"I wonder what your parents are going to do to you when they hear about this. Or better yet, the bishop."

Eli sagged against the pen. When he glanced back, the defensive look was gone. "I came to watch cows sell—see what the market was bringing. *Da* wants to sell part of the herd soon. I didn't come here asking for a fight."

"So why did it happen?"

Eli was silent. I grew impatient and pushed a little more. "Was it because of Hannah Kuhns?"

His body stiffened, confirming my suspicions.

"Arlo doesn't care about her—he's only using her. I simply told him to leave her be." The words shot out of his mouth.

I relaxed a little. Eli had the habit of picking the wrong girls to fall for. First Naomi and now Hannah. Both girls had a wild streak and a penchant for English boys, and both became pregnant.

"I understand that in your community freedom is not expected, but Hannah has the right to see whoever she wants to."

Eli stepped away from the pen and closer to me. "She's dealing with a lot right now—her sister's death and—"

He snapped his mouth closed. A shaky breath followed and my heart jumped. Perhaps Eli knew about the pregnancy.

"And then there's Jonas Peachey bothering her," Eli said.

"What does Jonas have to do with Hannah?" I leaned forward.

"He's a pervert—likes younger women, especially the ones who are kind of shy," Eli spit the words out. "He was hanging around Fannie before she died and now he's coming around Hannah."

My cell phone rang.

"Are you done with me?" Eli snapped.

Todd was walking away from the Arlo and his friends. I flicked my finger in their direction. "Avoid that crew. The next time something like this happens, you'll spend a night in jail," I warned.

Eli stared at me with hard eyes before he turned on his heels and was gone.

I brought the phone to my ear. "Hello."

"It was the remains of a fetus. I'm sending it for rushed lab work. There's a chance toxicology might pick up something, an indication of anything Marissa might have ingested to cause her to abort."

"Good work, Bobby," I said and hung up.

"I think I put the fear in those boys," Todd said when he reached me.

"Do you want to take a drive out to the settlement?" I asked, shoving my phone back into my pocket.

"What do we have?"

"I'm bringing Jonas Peachey in for formal questioning."

"Do we have enough for an arrest?" Todd rubbed his head.

"Are you willing to risk Hannah's life?"

When Todd and I stepped onto the Peachey's front porch, the late afternoon sun was still warm. Todd rapped on the door and I stared at the newly planted pansies in the flower garden below the porch. The dark brown dirt around them was clear of weeds and moist from a fresh watering. It amazed me how Amish women found the time to tend the plants when they had so many other things to do without modern conveniences to help them.

My gaze drifted to the wooden board snugly affixed into the window opening where the glass had been shot out. I was half surprised that it wasn't already replaced as quickly as the Amish attended to such things.

Esta opened the door. Her eyes passed quickly over Todd to settle on me. She smiled brightly.

"*Hullo*, Miss Serenity."

"Hi, Esta. Is your father home?" I asked. My skin crawled with my friendly deception. Esta wouldn't understand why her father was being taken away in a police cruiser. She'd already lost her mother.

When Ada Mae stepped up behind the girl, I relaxed a little. At least Ada Mae was there to pick up the pieces after Jonas was gone.

I met the woman's curious gaze. "I need to speak to Jonas."

"He's getting cleaned up. It shouldn't be long." She smiled. "I pulled fresh cinnamon rolls from the oven a moment ago." She bent down and said a few words in German to Esta, who ran back into the kitchen. "You must come in and do some sampling."

Ada Mae's complete comfortableness with two uniformed police officers at her door made the task worse. This situation was bad enough without the naivety of the Amish woman making me feel guilty. Then there was the smell of dough and cinnamon drifting out the front door. My stomach growled.

Todd began to go through the door. I stopped him with my hand in front of his chest. "We're on duty," I said with not much conviction.

Esta appeared in the doorway, holding a tray full of the cinnamon buns. The icing was melting right before my eyes and a soft steam rose.

"Oh, come on," Todd pleaded.

I flicked my hand at him, giving him the go ahead to take one. I controlled myself, though.

I wasn't going to eat one of Ada Mae's desserts right before I hauled her brother in for questioning. I ignored my watering mouth.

"I'm fine, thanks," I said.

Ada Mae's eyebrows rose in a hurt expression. I opened my mouth to explain why I wasn't jumping at a chance to devour her cinnamon rolls when Jonas stepped up behind her. His light blue eyes flared at the sight of me and Todd waiting on the porch. A lopsided smile appeared on his mouth.

"What brings you by, Sheriff?" he said as he lifted the suspenders over his shoulder to finish dressing.

"You need to come with us, Mr. Peachey. We have some formal questions for you," I said.

"Do I have a choice in the matter?" Jonas' eyes narrowed slightly.

"You can refuse. An hour from now, I'll be back with an arrest warrant. It's up to you. This can be easy or difficult. Your choice."

Jonas took a deep breath. "I'll go willingly." His voice was resigned.

Ada Mae rested her hand on Jonas' shoulder to stop him. Esta grasped her father's hand.

"Wait. What is this about? Why can't you ask your questions here?" Ada Mae implored.

Her expression was that of a deer caught in the headlights.

"We need to be in a controlled setting for the interview." I took a sharp breath, glancing at Jonas' calm face. "We have some questions about Fannie Kuhns and Marissa Gingerich."

Jonas' lips thinned and his cheek twitched.

Ada Mae exclaimed, "I don't understand. Marissa is the simple woman back in Ohio. What does she have to do with any of this?"

I looked at Jonas, gesturing at him. "Jonas knows why."

Jonas didn't speak. His one brow rose, acknowledging me, then he turned to his sister and daughter.

"I'll be back soon. Don't worry. I am in the Lord's hands. He will protect me." He kissed Esta on the top of the head and made eye contact with Ada Mae briefly before he stepped away from them, walking past us to the car.

Todd shrugged at me and followed Jonas.

I turned to go, but Ada Mae's hand snaked out, grasping my arm. She quickly let go.

"Jonas is no criminal. He has spent his entire adult life helping people. It isn't in him to harm another." She took a shaky breath. "I'll pray for him—and you, Sheriff."

Ada Mae backed away, closing the door. The sudden quiet on the porch felt significant. I shook the feeling away, remembering Marissa's sad song by the pond. Ada Mae was wrong. Jonas definitely had the capability to harm others. And he had.

23

SERENITY

"I didn't think you were officially starting the job for a few more weeks," I commented, not looking at Elayne.

We were both staring through the one-way mirror at Jonas. He sat in the chair, occasionally closing his eyes and moving his mouth in what I assumed to be prayer.

Elayne flicked her hair over her shoulder. She inclined her head. "After talking to Irene, I was drawn into Fannie's case, and it's not just because I used to be Amish. The situation is strange. Amish girls usually don't become pregnant before they're married. Her sudden death is even more unusual."

I took a breath and looked at Elayne. She stood tall in heels that were at least four inches high. Her skirt was short, but appropriate. The purple blouse she wore was the only bright thing in the drab, gray room. Her brown gaze met mine and her brow lifted.

"Did Bobby fill you in on Marissa Gingerich?" I trusted Bobby. He was discreet. Elayne would eventually be privy to all the evidence anyway, and she was supposed to be on our side.

As we quietly sized each other up, wariness closed in on me. This woman would be a thorn in my side for a long time to come. I had to find a way to put my personal emotions aside and work with her.

"Yes, he did." Her gaze shifted to Jonas, her face softening. "I remember Marissa. Not well, but I do recall seeing her at a few of the weddings my family attended in Ohio. She was a curiosity back then. She was pretty enough and fully functional. If she didn't open her mouth, a person could be fooled into thinking she was normal." Elayne swallowed. "The boys alternated between teasing her and taking advantage of her. I'm not surprised she became pregnant. Even among the Amish, there are predators, and she was an easy target." She nodded at Jonas. "But I never would have guessed that it would be him."

Her tone told me that even though she was surprised, she believed my theory. Something about her agreeableness opened me up. I'd always dislike her for her connections to Daniel and her overly flirtatious ways, but perhaps I could respect her on a professional level.

"Marissa was very clear that he was the one she'd been fooling around with. She didn't mention anyone else," I said.

"A good defense attorney will have a field day with her mental disabilities, though." Her eyes narrowed, and her voice dropped. "We have to make sure we have a strong case before we move forward. We don't want that man to get away with it."

I nodded. "Do you want to join me for the interrogation?"

"I wouldn't miss it," she replied, not surprising me at all.

I seated myself in front of Jonas. Elayne chose to stand to my left. She had a notepad in her hands, a pen poised above the paper.

Jonas stared back at me. I couldn't help remembering his wild look as he prayed for Mervin and the poisoned girls. I felt the heavy, oppressive air that had surrounded Mervin so unnaturally. I stopped myself from shivering, wiping the memory away.

"How long did you have a secret relationship with Marissa Gingerich before she became pregnant?"

"Pregnant?" Jonas' eyes widened. He glanced between me and Elayne and leaned over the table. In barely a whisper, he said, "She was pregnant?"

I sat up straighter and looked at Elayne. She shrugged and her lips pressed together in a thin line.

I'd done a lot of interrogations. Most of the time, the perp lied outright or lied in a roundabout way, skirting the questions. Rarely was someone immediately contrite. As much as I didn't want to see it on Jonas' face, he was shocked, maybe even upset, about Marissa's pregnancy.

Drawing on my own psychological training and pushing aside Jonas' reaction, I took a breath and continued with the questioning.

"Did you have intercourse with Marisa Gingerich?"

Jonas' face reddened, but he didn't look away. "Yes, I did."

His straightforwardness was unsettling, making goosebumps rise on my arms.

"So you agree that the fetus that I recovered from beside the pond at the Gingerich household could in fact be yours?"

Jonas nodded. "It's a possibility." He ran a hand through his black beard, dropping his head. "I never meant to cause her pain. I would have taken her as my wife, if—" He stopped abruptly.

"If what?" I urged. When he remained silent, I added, "You're a God fearing man, aren't you?"

"Of course."

"The truth will eventually come out. It's better to be honest. If you try to deceive us, you might find yourself living away from your family for a very long time."

Jonas still didn't speak. He was either stubborn or worried about what he almost said.

Elayne placed her hands on the table. When she spoke, it was in her birth language. I didn't understand her words, but the response Jonas had was telling. His eyes moistened. He dabbed the wetness away with his sleeve.

He faced me again. "Ada Mae wouldn't allow it. She said it would be a disgrace to our family for me to marry a simpleton."

I rolled his words over in my mind. Ada Mae seemed to be the obedient sister. But maybe it was a ruse. Perhaps she was the one who ruled Jonas. The thought was unsettling.

"You're a grown man. You can marry whomever you want. Why would you listen to your sister?"

Jonas had a faraway look on his face. "Ada Mae is very smart. Like Momma, she always knows what to do."

I glanced at Elayne. She frowned, but allowed me to continue with the questioning.

"What about Fannie Kuhns? Were you going to marry her, too?"

Jonas sat back, his eyes even wider. "What are you talking about?" He looked at Elayne. "*Ime familye wag?* No."

"Weren't you having sex with Fannie?" I plowed on.

"Of course not. I treated her mother for the asthma and I brought herbal remedies to her for stomach aches and such. There was nothing between us."

My gut was telling me that he spoke the truth or at least what he believed was the truth. But then what the hell was going on?

I took a chance, attempting to push the man further. "Marissa and Fannie had connections to you. You admit that one of them could have been pregnant with your child. They both miscarried. Fannie even died. Your wife died unexpectedly while delivering Esta, and even your mother died in the birthing bed." I leaned back in the chair. "You're the medicine man. What do you think happened to the women?"

A tremor passed over Jonas. His face paled.

"I will say no more on the matter," Jonas said. His blue eyes glistened with unshed tears.

When we were back in the observation room, I turned to Elayne, who was staring off into space, her mouth slightly agape.

"I don't have enough to hold him."

"No, you don't," Elayne confirmed, meeting my gaze. "Do you think he's telling the truth?"

"I do, which leaves me with not a lot to go on in this investigation." I sighed.

The door opened and Daniel stepped into the room. Bobby was two steps behind him.

Daniel ignored Elayne, his gaze landing squarely on me. "We have a problem," he stated. "Eli seems to have disappeared."

Damn.

"There's more," Bobby spoke up. "I have the lab results back on the fetus. There were traces of tansy ragwort in the tissue. Along with peppermint."

"Peppermint?" I turned to look at Jonas through the window. He was praying again. I watched his mouth moving. Peppermint. Peppermint. My mind clicked, and my heart dropped into my belly.

I met Daniel's eyes with a sense of desperation. "We need to hurry." I paused, motioning to Bobby. "You better join us on this one."

Bobby nodded curtly as he removed his glasses, sticking them into his oversized pants pocket. Elayne stepped in front of me. "What do you want me to do?"

"Keep Jonas occupied until you hear from me."

I only hoped I was wrong about this one.

24

SERENITY

"Maybe Jonas is telling the truth," Daniel said as he turned into the Bender's driveway.

"That he wanted to marry Marissa?" I snorted. "I doubt it. He took advantage of her. He's a predator."

"The Amish see things differently than we do. It might not be what it seems," Daniel said.

I glared at him. "Just because Jonas has rock-star status in the community doesn't give him free rein to sleep with whomever he wants. Surely, even you can see that."

"I agree, but I don't see how you're going to pin Fannie's death on him."

"I'm failing to see the connection myself," Bobby mumbled in the backseat.

A hundred thoughts ran through my mind at once. I almost had it figured out, but parts of the puzzle were still missing. One thing I knew for sure, Hannah's life and possibly even Eli's were in danger.

Several chickens flapped their tan wings, squawking, and jumped away from Daniel's Jeep as he pulled up beside the barn. Katherine crossed the barnyard at a jog, stopping out-side my open window. She leaned in.

"*Danki*, for coming. I didn't know what to do. Joseph is out of town, inquiring about a team of horses for sale and I couldn't reach him," Katherine said. Her usually pale skin was flushed and several strands of dark hair stuck out from under her cap in disarray. Two small children peeked around the barn door at us.

"What's going on?" I asked.

"Eli didn't sleep in his bed last night." Katherine frowned and then sighed. "The boy has a rebellious streak, but he wouldn't be gone from home when he knew his father was away. Then there are the problems he's been having with those English boys. I worry about him."

Daniel's lips were pinched, but he didn't say anything.

"He's eighteen years old, a grown man. It's not my business to hunt down young men." When I met her gaze, there were tears in her eyes. I buckled. "But under the circumstances, I'll do what I can," I offered. "Do you have any idea where he might be?"

Katherine looked away. The sky was darkening to a slate gray to the west. A flash of lightning zigzagged across the sky. The sun sliced through the clouds above our heads, making the approach of the impending storm less threatening. A low rumble rolled through the clouds.

Katherine's lips quivered. A battle seemed to be raging inside of her as if she didn't know how honest to be with me.

She turned back with hard eyes that took me by surprise.

"Best pay Hannah Kuhns a visit. Eli took a liking to the girl some months ago." She shook her head. "I warned him against it. That girl has the same restless spirit that Naomi had. Nothing but trouble can come from falling in love with her, I told him." A wispy smile touched her lips. "But sons don't listen to their mothers. Do they, Daniel?"

Daniel chuckled, the sound sad. "We don't always have control over who we fall in love with." He glanced at me.

Isn't that just the damn truth.

"We'll find him, Katherine. Don't worry," I assured her.

After all the experiences I'd had with the Amish people, I wasn't willing to bet on my declaration, though.

As we turned out of Katherine's driveway, the last bit of sunshine disappeared behind a fast moving, dark cloud. I peered up, wondering how much time we had before it poured.

"I feel for Katherine. Eli is a handful."

Daniel shrugged. "He's just trying to figure out where he belongs. Unfortunately, he's searching for that place with a girl, and not in himself."

"You talk as if you're speaking from experience," I commented.

"I am. I made the biggest mistake of my life because of a girl. Strangely, deep down, I knew it at the time, but I couldn't help myself. It's the same for Eli."

Another flash of lightning coursed across the sky and I blinked. A few seconds later the low booming vibrated the Jeep. A few drops of rain splattered the windshield.

"If you hadn't made that mistake, you probably would be married to that Amish girl, Rosetta, and have a herd of children to call your own." I tried not to sound spiteful, but it hurt saying it.

Daniel smiled faintly. The rain drops were multiplying and a sudden *swoosh* of wind rained a mass of swirling leaves against the Jeep.

"That's not true. I was destined to leave the Amish. I realize that now. I just wish it hadn't been over a girl. Maybe if my parents had understood that the Plain ways weren't for me, they would have accepted my departure easier." He shrugged. "It might have been same, though. I'll never know."

"When did you know that being Amish wasn't for you?" Bobby asked. His voice startled me. I had forgotten all about him in the backseat.

Daniel barked out a laugh as the rain began pounding the Jeep. "It was after a ball game. I must have been about sixteen at the time. I was driving Da's buggy in a procession of other buggies leaving the game. Several of my friends, including Lester, were with me. We turned onto State Route Forty-Eight, a shortcut back to one of the boy's farm. Several other buggies went with us. By that time, we were first in line."

He took a quick breath and I found that I was holding my own.

"I heard the tires screeching and the horn blaring before I looked in the side-view mirror. A semi-truck had gone sideways, careening across the roadway. It smashed into the last buggy in line." Daniel cleared his throat. "I saw the horse go down under the trailer. The buggy resembled a piece of crumbled black paper. Lester and I were the first to reach what was left of it. The horse's body was broken apart, its legs snapped in two. It took its dying breath in my hands. Two of the three girls riding in the buggy were thrown clear. One died on the side of the road and the other died later in the hospital. The third girl was an unrecognizable pile of blue material and blood trapped beneath the wreckage. I held the one girl's hand until the ambulance arrived. She kept mumbling that it hurt, over and over." He met my gaze. "After that, every time I drove a buggy, my stomach clenched. I remember thinking, *how can I raise a family into such a dangerous way of life?*"

A louder boom of thunder erupted. As I searched out the rain streaked window, the fields filled with puddles. Tree leaves were flipped and glistening. I sniffed, trying to erase the terrible image that Daniel's words inspired.

"Lester remained Amish," I remarked.

"The Amish have a Calvinist approach to life. If God intends for something to happen, there's no stopping it. Lester believes it and so do my sister and parents. I don't share the sentiment, and I didn't back then. It was unreasonable to me to put myself into such jeopardy on a daily basis, and then there were all the rules that went against my way of thinking, too. I was a lot like Eli—a rebellious spirit, looking for a way out."

A gust of wind shook the Jeep. Daniel slowed the vehicle. He reached across the seat with an open hand. I grasped it.

"How are you feeling?" Daniel's voice was almost too low to hear above the driving rain.

Heat flared across my cheeks and I turned my head away, hoping Bobby hadn't seen. He was a sharp old man. If Daniel wasn't careful, Bobby would guess about the possible pregnancy. That was the last thing I needed at the moment. I licked my lips. I'd been too distracted lately to think much about the possibility that I was pregnant. It was a fantastical idea, one that I didn't want to dwell on.

Glancing sideways, I saw the concern in Daniel's eyes.

I swallowed. "One crisis at a time. I promise, I'll focus on that after we get this Amish business cleared up."

Daniel smiled. "I'd hardly call it a crisis."

I rolled my eyes. That Daniel seemed to be hoping for a positive pregnancy test was about as unnerving as the fact that I needed to take one in the first place.

The Kuhns' farm was blurry through the pouring rain. A dozen or more horses and buggies were parked in the driveway. I felt sorry for the horses. Their heads were dropped into the driving rain. Here and there were spots of brightness from the women's dresses, but otherwise the place was a sheet of gray wetness on the hill.

"Fannie's funeral is today," I mumbled.

"So it seems." Daniel parked and leaned over. "Do you still want to go in there?"

My heart pounded at the sight of a dozen or so Amish men standing in the open doorway of the barn we passed. Their beards were the only hint of color amidst the black of their clothing. I couldn't help but think back to the scene in the abandoned barn the previous fall. That same group of Amish men had held me captive while they attempted to carry out their own form of vigilante justice.

"We have no choice. Time might be against us," I said, remembering the desperate look on Hannah's face. I eyed the backseat. Bobby's fingers played with his mustache. His eyes were keen. "Stay here, Bobby."

"Considering the weather conditions, I won't argue with you," Bobby replied.

We dashed through the rain to the porch. The patter of a million darts on the tin roof blasted my ears as I rapped on the door. A woman I didn't know peeked through the doorway. She disappeared, seeking out Irene, I assumed.

The quiet drone of conversation coming from the room was barely noticeable above the building storm. Another flash lit the sky. A cold gust of wet wind swept through the porch.

When I turned back to the door, Irene was standing there. "Sheriff?" Irene lifted her chin.

"I'd like to speak to Hannah."

A tear dripped from Irene's eye. She wiped it away. "She's not here."

The breath caught in my throat. "Do you know where she is?"

"She left a few hours ago—said she wanted to be alone. I didn't stop her. Fannie's death has been difficult on her." She glanced over my shoulder at the water soaked world. "I thought she'd be home by now, to show respect for her sister."

I took a step back. "I'm sorry, I know this isn't the best time, but when she returns, will you have her call me?" I handed Irene another one of my business cards, in case the first one had been lost.

She nodded, slipping back through the door. From the corner of my eye, I saw a flash of color—pinkish—in the loft window of the smaller barn standing off by itself. It might have been my imagination, but the way my stomach twisted, I didn't think so.

Pushing my hat further down on my head, I motioned for Daniel to follow. Luckily, the rain was keeping the Amish people inside the house or under cover in the larger barn beside the house. As the rain pelted down on us, we ran across the field. A bright flash, joined by a clap of thunder, made me jump, but I kept running.

Daniel stayed close beside me, not wasting time to ask what the hell I was doing.

With a surge of strength, I pushed my legs faster until I reached the barn door. Daniel leaned over me, pushing it open. We stepped into the darkness of the aisle to be greeted by the dank smell of old wood and dirt. Unlike most Amish barns, this one was cluttered with rusty farm machinery that didn't look like it had been used in a while. A thick coating of dust covered everything. I sneezed before I could stop myself. So much for sneaking up on anyone.

Daniel shook the water from his hair and looked down at me expectantly. I pointed at the loft. Daniel nodded and motioned me to get behind him. I relented. The chances of someone sneaking up on us were just as good as a threat coming from ahead. I reached inside my jacket, pulling my gun out. I raised it in front of me. When Daniel glanced over his shoulder, his eyes widened.

I shrugged. *I'll never be unprepared in an Amish barn again.*

Daniel opened the narrow wooden door. The steps were steep and they creaked loudly as he crept up them. I took the steps as lightly as I could.

When he reached the opening into the loft, he paused, squinting into the shadowed room. He glanced at me, giving me the thumbs up before he took the last steps into the loft. I followed.

The smell of moldy hay and stale air assaulted my nose. Dim light shone in through the small, narrow windows. Dust particles floated in the air. I waved in front of me in an attempt to clear a path. I looked down and noticed the foot prints on the floor.

"Show yourself. Do it nice and easy," I called out.

There was a shuffling sound in the corner. I aimed my gun, not taking any chances.

When they came out from behind the hay bales, their hands were raised and their faces were long. They weren't the faces I was expecting to see at all.

I lowered my gun, returning it to its holster. Daniel breathed out a sigh.

"What are you two doing up here?" I demanded.

I caught a glimpse of Daniel shaking his head, but I ignored him.

Mervin took a step closer to Verna. He finally found his voice, but he looked at Daniel instead of me. "We don't get to spend any time together. We just wanted to talk."

Verna's face flushed a deeper red and I felt like a complete idiot.

Daniel touched my arm. "Come on," he urged, nudging me towards the steps.

I was about to go with him when Verna's light blue eyes met mine. I stopped. "Have you seen Hannah Kuhns' today?"

Verna glanced at Mervin. He nodded for her to answer. "Yes. She came to see my aunt this morning."

My brow knitted together. Another piece of the puzzle fell into place.

I turned away from the teenagers, taking the steps down to the first floor in a hurry.

I was afraid that no matter how fast I ran, I would be too late.

25

SERENITY

I knocked on the door again, this time harder. When no one answered, I looked at Daniel.

"We need to get into this house," I said.

Daniel whirled and jogged to the Jeep. The rain was a steady pattering, instead of a deluge, but the sky flashed intermittently and thunder rolled overhead. Daniel returned a moment later with a hammer.

Bobby and I stepped back as Daniel hooked the claw end of the hammer around the edge of the board that sealed the broken window and pulled. The board popped free. I had my gun out as I stepped through the opening into the kitchen in front of Daniel and Bobby. The scents of maple and bacon were heavy in the air. Dirty skillets were carelessly pushed aside on the countertop. Plates of half eaten food littered the table.

I paused to listen. The rain hitting the tin roof was loud enough to disguise most random noises and I inwardly cursed the storm's timing.

"You two take the upstairs. I'll hit the basement," I whispered.

"I think we should stay together," Daniel argued, taking a step closer.

"No time," I told him. He frowned, but when Bobby left the kitchen, following my orders, he shook his head and followed the coroner into the hallway.

I turned the knob on the door I thought led to the basement, opening it carefully. Stairs disappeared into darkness, proving me right.

With no time to hesitate, I went down the steps, moving sideways and holding my gun up and ready. Blinking, my eyes adjusted to the darkness. I took a breath before I turned the corner when I reached the last step.

Bundles of dried plants hung from the rafters and a table in the center of the room held assorted piles of seeds, leaves and bottles. The room brightened and a crash of thunder followed. I didn't see anyone.

My heart pounded frantically. Jonas' statement about Ada Mae not allowing him to marry Marissa repeated in my head. *The peppermint makes it taste better. It's my special ingredient.* Robyn drank tea and died in childbirth. Fannie drank the tea and died. But Marissa didn't die—although she very well might have.

"Why are you here?" Ada Mae's voice rang out behind me.

I jumped, turning at the same time and pointing my gun at her.

"You know why. You're the one person who's connected to everyone who's died or miscarried," I accused. "Where's Hannah?"

Ada Mae stared calmly back at me as if the gun aimed at her didn't matter.

"The girl came to me looking for aid. Not the other way around," Ada Mae replied.

"Where is she?" I lowered my voice, taking a step towards the Amish woman.

"It's too late." Ada Mae frowned. "The silly girl shouldn't have flirted with Jonas. He's weak in the flesh. I couldn't let her slutty ways affect him. Look at what her sister already did."

"No, Ada Mae. Fannie was involved with a young English man. Hannah and Eli were a couple. Neither one of those girls slept with Jonas," I tried to convince her.

Ada Mae's eyes narrowed. There was a touch of madness in them I hadn't seen before.

"I don't believe you," she snapped.

The urgency to find Hannah was tempered by the keen desire to hear the woman out, to try to understand why she'd done the things she had.

"It's not too late. You have the ability to help Hannah." I softened my voice. "You have a gift, Ada Mae, a gift to help people, not hurt them."

"I do. But my purpose in life has always been to protect my brother—to care for him and his children. That's my priority." She smiled. "He was mine way before he was Robyn's or Marissa's, Fannie's or Hannah's. When we were children, it was me he loved. Me who he kissed." She glanced down in embarrassment. "Oh, I knew that it was wrong in the eyes of our Lord, but I didn't care."

"Jonas cared, didn't he? He put a stop to it, but you couldn't stand losing him. Is that why you killed Robyn? You were recently widowed and alone at the time. Did the desire to be with your brother again drive you to do the unthinkable?"

It was then that I noticed the lighter in her hand and got a whiff of the rotten egg gas scent. I stalled my movement. It dawned on me the reason why the woman, who had kept her secrets her entire life, was now freeing herself of them.

"It wasn't easy. She was the mother of my nieces. Those children should have been mine all along." Ada Mae frowned.

I swallowed, watching her hand waver in the air. I was judging the distance to her and how fast I could run when another voice spoke up behind me. I sucked in a breath of surprise.

"So it was *you* who killed my dear sister," the bishop said. "When did your soul become infected with the poison of the devil? Was it when you killed your mother?"

I didn't dare look the bishop's way. I couldn't take my eyes from Ada Mae. The expression that widened her face was sickly mesmerizing.

"And how would you know of that, *Aaron Esch*?" Ada Mae said the name with distaste, as if she'd bitten into a piece of bitter fruit.

"Many years ago Wilma Gingerich told me of the tea that your mother drank before she and her child died in the birthing bed. Wilma had no proof that it was the tea that killed them, but she suspected as much. She'd seen enough births to know when something was amiss. That's why I suspected Jonas' involvement in Robyn's death. It wasn't until Daniel spoke to his mother about the contents of the tea that took Fannie's life that I made the connection to you."

He took another step into the basement and my hand shot up. "Stop there, Bishop."

"Momma wasn't meant to die. I was young and inexperienced about the combination of certain herbs at the time. She was a frail woman. I thought another delivery at her age would kill her. I mixed the ingredients, hoping to force her menses on her, to bleed the baby out. But the bleeding was too much."

She paused. "That's how I learned how to make a potion to kill."

I took a quick breath. "Why didn't you kill Marissa then?"

"She should have died. Maybe she didn't drink enough of the tea. It doesn't matter. I'll stand trial before my Lord at his altar."

"Please don't," I whispered, shifting my aim to Ada Mae's head, but knew that even if I could stop her from striking the lighter, the gunshot blast would ignite the gas.

Ada Mae raised the lighter.

Indecision rushed through me. Stomping on the stairs made Ada Mae glance away.

"You killed her—killed Hannah," Eli choked out.

He raised a rifle. The bishop scrambled for Eli's gun, but missed.

The gunshot echoed a split second before the explosion ripped through my senses.

26

DANIEL

I didn't like parting from Serenity, but time wasn't in abundance. Breaking into two groups made the most sense. Serenity was also the sheriff. I already knew she could take care of herself, and part of me refused to believe the Peacheys posed any real danger to anyone. Jonas was sitting in the interrogation room back at the station. Surely we weren't walking into anything more troubling than catching Hannah and Eli in the middle of acting out against the rules of their society.

Bobby didn't feel the same way. When I glanced at him, his eyes darted back and forth. Thunder rumbled, vibrating the house, and yet the creaking on the floor boards from our feet boomed louder in my ears. Lightning flashed and a louder clap sounded. I took advantage of the noise and hurried up the remaining steps.

I held my breath. Wandering around a home I wasn't invited into wasn't something I was used to.

I peeked into the first doorway. Only a neatly made bed and a dresser in the corner were there. Bobby went around me to look into the second doorway. I silently cursed that he'd gone ahead. If there was any kind of threat, I didn't know what the old coroner was going to do about it.

When Bobby disappeared into the room, I lengthened my stride, following him.

Hannah was lying on the bed. Eli leaned over her, rubbing her forehead.

"Did she drink tea?" Bobby belted out, rushing to the bedside faster than I would have thought possible. He picked up an empty cup from the nightstand and sniffed it.

"She did. Ada Mae gave it to her. Hannah wanted to rid herself of our baby—she done it on purpose," Eli exclaimed. He stood, taking a step backward. His face was distorted in grief.

Bobby grimaced at the cup and carefully set it back down. He leaned over Hannah.

"Sweetheart, let me look at your eyes," he coaxed.

Hannah turned to him. As Bobby spread her eyes wider with his fingertips, sweat drops slid down the side of her ashen face.

Bobby shot me a look. "We don't have much time. She needs emergency care. I'm afraid that if we wait for an ambulance, it will be too late."

"I didn't want to kill the baby—but I didn't know—didn't know if it was Eli's or Arlo's." Hannah grabbed Bobby's wrist with a sudden show of strength. "Arlo forced himself on me. He was showing attention to Fannie, then one day, he began hounding me. I told him no. But he wouldn't listen..." Her words trailed off into wet tears and sniffing.

Eli dropped onto the bed, grasping her face in his hands. "I would have helped you through it, Hannah. You should have trusted me. It's not your fault what Arlo did to you, and it's not the baby's fault, either."

The maturity in Eli's voice startled me. The kid had come a long way since he'd lost Naomi's love to Serenity's nephew. Looking down on the tortured scene, I couldn't help wondering about his bad luck with women.

"All right. Bobby, call the hospital and tell them we're on our way with the patient. Fill them in on whatever they need to know." I met Eli's fearful eyes. "Let me help her, Eli."

He rubbed his hands through his hair with a tug and groaned, but moved aside.

I slipped my hand under Hannah's back and legs, lifting her from the bed. The solidness of her weight and the limpness of her body lengthened my stride. I heard Bobby behind me, talking on the phone. I remained hopeful that we'd make it to the hospital in time to save the girl, but seeing the blood spreading on Hannah's dress made me fear that the baby was already lost.

"Serenity, come on! I found them!" I shouted, fearing she was already searching the barn.

Eli jumped in front of me and opened the door. I barely paused on the porch before taking the steps two at a time. I darted into the rain as the sky lightened around us. The boom of thunder was directly overhead.

Clip clops echoed above the storm and I raised my head into the rain to see a buggy being pulled at a pounding trot up the driveway. The horse threw its head with the thunder, its eyes wide with terror. The buggy pulled alongside us as I placed Hannah in the backseat of the Jeep. She slumped over, unconscious.

Eli grabbed the horse's reins, struggling to control it. Aaron Esch was the first out of the buggy. Father and Ma jumped out after him. I paused, startled by their appearance.

The rain pelted down on Ma, but she ignored it. Her eyes flashed with the lightning when she turned to me. "How long since she ingested the poisons?" she called out to be heard above the wind.

Eli moved closer, still holding onto the horse. "When I found her, she said it had only been about an hour. So maybe an hour and a half in total."

Ma's face dropped into a frown. "We may be too late then," she muttered.

Bobby squeezed in and faced Ma. "I believe she ingested the same herbs that Fannie did. Tansy ragwort, pennyroyal, parsley, and peppermint. We need to get her to the emergency room. She's already bleeding."

Ma pulled a jar from her pocket. Dark liquid sloshed around inside of it. "This might slow the bleeding." Her gaze didn't waiver as she looked at Bobby. "If there's any hope, she needs it now."

Bobby took a breath and nodded, moving aside so Ma could climb into the back seat with Hannah. My eyes popped wide when Ma slapped Hannah's cheek.

"Wake up, Hannah. You must drink this." Ma looked at Bobby over her shoulder. "Go to the other side and hold her up."

Bobby did as he was told. Another clap of thunder rolled over us. I glanced up to watch the gray clouds billowing across the sky with the harsh wind. Father stood stoically in the rain beside me.

"Where's Aaron?" I asked Father.

Father raised his shoulders, shrugging. I looked back at the house. Shifting on my feet, my stomach clenched. *Where's Serenity?*

I was turning to go back to the house to search for her when Ma's voice rose above the gusts of wind. When I looked back, her eyes were closed. She had one hand on Hannah's head and another above her. The jar lay on the ground beside the Jeep, empty.

The chanting brought me back to another place and time. *I was in my childhood yard. Lester's head was resting in my lap. Ma was speaking the same strange words. Words I didn't understand. Words that scared me.*

As if we were in the eye of a hurricane, the storm diminished around us. The rain lessened to a drizzle and the clouds lifted, revealing blue sky. The wind died down to a stiff, cool breeze. I held my breath, unable to tear my eyes away from the three people huddled together in the small space at the back of my Jeep.

Ma's voice was a continuous rambling that rose and fell with the wind. Bobby's eyes were closed, too. His mouth moved in his own silent praying. Hannah's eyes were the only ones open. They shone out of her face with a brilliance all their own, and they were terrified.

"I don't want to die," she cried out.

A coughing fit overtook Hannah. Her body rocked violently and she doubled over in Bobby's arms. Bobby's eyes met mine and they glinted with unshed tears. Ma didn't slow her chanting. Hannah lay still.

I heard the sloshing through the puddles before I turned my head. Eli was running to the house. The horse jumped into a half rear and Father grabbed for the reins to steady the animal.

I looked back into the Jeep. Hannah wasn't breathing. Her head lolled back on Bobby's shoulder and her skin was deathly white.

The same heavy stillness overtook the air that I'd felt when Lester had stopped breathing and Mervin had gulped for breath. I took a shuddering breath and closed my eyes. Whatever it was shouldn't be seen.

With my eyes squeezed tightly together, I began praying. Praying for Hannah and Serenity, even my own soul. There wasn't any rhyme or reason to the words in my head. They poured out from my terrified heart.

The wind settled. All was quiet. The world seemed to be waiting, as if drawing in a deep breath.

Several long seconds passed. Hannah lurched forward, sucking in a gulp of air. Ma held onto her, crying a triumphant thank you to the heavens, and sinking back down to murmur soothing words in our native tongue to Hannah.

Bobby breathed, "Praise God."

The wind whipped back up and rain pelted us from the sky once again.

"We best get her to the hospital," Bobby called out.

I hesitated, looking back at the house. Time was of the essence. Hannah needed more medical help, but I didn't want to leave Serenity. Why wasn't she here?

Ma lifted her face, pale and tight with fear. "Oh, no," she whispered.

The explosion blasted in my ears and a shock of heat hit me, knocking me into the side of the Jeep. It took everything Father had to hold onto the horse as it bolted sideways.

When I opened my eyes, the left side of the Peachey house was a pile of burning rubble. Red hot flames flicked into the air, battling with the downpour for supremacy.

Ma's hand grasped my arm.

"I'm so sorry, son."

I pulled away from her and ran towards the inferno and sickening smoke.

"Serenity!"

27

SERENITY

When I finally had the nerve to open my eyes, clumps of debris were burning around me. The grass was scorched black and a thick cloud of smoke blotted out the sky. I lifted my face to the rain, thankful for its cold wetness. The sound of the howling wind and booming thunder were music to my ears. I was alive, and I could wiggle all my toes and fingers.

With concentrated effort, I pushed up on my elbows to take a better look at the scene. The sharp pain that shot through my leg rolled me backward onto smoldering splinters of wood. I shimmied sideways on my back to avoid being burnt. Drawing in a sharp breath, I swallowed and lifted my head to see my leg. A large portion of the jeans were gone and a swath of shredded, black skin was exposed. Hot bile rose in my throat and I quickly turned away, forcing my throat to swallow. *It could have been worse,* I tried to convince myself.

Lifting my chin, I gazed around at the devastation. I'd been thrown clear of the brunt of the burning wreckage. The sight of only half of the house standing made me blink. *How did I survive that?* A cloud of smoke puffed off the nearest pile in my direction, making me cough. The movement caused throbbing in a hundred places on my body.

My injuries flitted from my mind when I saw lavender material flapping in the wind. This time when I pushed up, I took a deep breath and ignored the stinging pain. It was Ada Mae—at least what was left of her. My gaze swept over her glassy eyes and bloody dress. A broken board jutted from her stomach, pointing straight to the sky. Her mouth gaped open. I wondered if she'd had a chance to ask forgiveness for her evil deeds before she died. The thought made me shiver.

The flash of white about twenty yards away stilled my heart. The bishop's beard.

I was struggling to rise when Daniel clasped my shoulders. He held me in place, dropping in front of me. A gust of wind blanketed us with pelting rain. Daniel leaned in closer to shield me from the onslaught.

His wide, brown eyes searched mine. "Are you all right? Speak to me. Say something," Daniel ordered with panic in his voice.

"I'm okay, I think." My voice was raspy to my ears. "Except my left leg." When Daniel's eyes shot downwards, I added, "It's not broken, just burned and cut up pretty bad."

I nodded towards Ada Mae's body. "She's wasn't so lucky. I think the bishop is over there," I said, motioning with a weak flick of my hand.

Bobby plopped down beside us, forcing Daniel to lean back. "Thank the Lord above you're alive." He grasped my wrist, taking my pulse and searching my eyes. "You're like a cat—more lives than you know what to do with," he muttered, sounding grumpy, but there was no mistaking his wide smile. He was happy to see me.

Daniel met my gaze, his face grim. I nodded. He rose and touched my head before he left. Bobby wrapped his coat around my injured leg and chattered about the scope of the blast and the miracle of my survival, but I barely listened. My gaze followed Daniel as he gingerly made his way through the burning debris to reach the bishop. I help my breath, fearing the worst.

For several unbearable seconds, Daniel hovered over the bishop. The old man's beard rose and fell with the wind. The rain shifted to a sprinkle. I blinked, trying to clear my eyes.

I exhaled loudly and Bobby paused to look in the same direction. Daniel was helping Aaron Esch to his feet. The bishop clung to Daniel's side as Daniel dragged him away from the house and closer to me. A sizzling crash turned all our heads. Another portion of the house collapsed, sending flames and smoke shooting high in the sky. I was sure the billowing cloud could be seen from miles away.

"Was anyone else in there?" Bobby breathed.

I tilted my head to listen. The sound of distant hoof beats on the pavement echoed in my ears. They were coming. The entire community was on their way.

"Eli," I whispered. "Eli was."

Daniel sucked in a breath and laid the bishop down beside me.

"Find him." The bishop waved Daniel away. His voice was scratchy and shaky, but the usual authority was unmistakable.

Daniel did as he was told, abandoning the bishop to search through the wreckage.

Bobby moved over to the bishop. "All things considered, you don't look so bad," Bobby teased. He gently probed the man's many injuries without asking permission. Bobby was a coroner, not a doctor, but he was the most qualified medical personnel we had at the moment.

"Such a shame," the bishop mumbled. "So much needless death—so much evil."

I looked at him, meeting his gaze. "At least you have closure. You finally know what happened to your sister, and Ada Mae is dead."

The bishop shook his head defiantly. "I didn't wish to see her punished in such a way. She was a troubled woman. The devil worked his mischief in her weak mind. She was as much a victim as Robyn and Fannie." He took a steady breath. "I forgive her sins."

I was about to respond, to chastise the bishop for his ignorance, when the man closed his eyes and dropped his head, praying.

Bobby shot me a warning look. I sighed and shrugged. Maybe I was jealous that my heart wasn't so forgiving. Three women had died needlessly. Sure, Ada Mae's mother might have been an accident, but Ada Mae had murdered Robyn and Fannie. Maybe Hannah was dead too, and she tried to do the same to Marissa. Being messed up in the head didn't give a person the right to take a person's life. It wasn't my job to pardon criminals. I brought justice to the victims.

But glancing at the bishop's peaceful face, still in silent prayer, I had to respect his ability to let go of a grudge. It was probably much healthier in the long run.

While Bobby was talking on his cell phone to central dispatch, I took the opportunity to rise on shaky legs. Clenching my teeth through the pain, I limped through the wreckage. I stepped over shards of glass, crumpled tin and splintered, smoldering wood. The rain stopped. There were breaks in the dark clouds, sending slivers of sun shining down. I made my way around the upside-down wood-burning stove lying in the yard and past one of the kitchen chairs hanging in the branches of a scorched tree.

When I saw Daniel kneeling on the ground, the breath caught in my throat. I sped up, dragging my wounded leg until I reached him. Eli was there. Part of the roof was on top of his hips and legs. His right arm was bent back grotesquely. The other one was completely gone.

I flopped down in the charred grass beside Daniel and leaned in close to Eli's face. My eyes widened when his flicked open. They blinked and settled on me. He made a scrappy, hissing sound.

I dropped my ear to his mouth to hear him.

"Did...Hannah...die?" he wheezed.

I glanced up at Daniel, my heart pounding even harder. "Where's Hannah?"

Daniel leaned over me, answering Eli. "She's going to be all right. My mother arrived and took care of her. She healed Hannah."

"Baby?" Eli struggled to get the word out. His blue eyes were becoming unfocused. I knew that look. I took a deep breath and blew it out slowly.

"I don't know for sure, but I think she lost it," Daniel said in a steady voice.

Eli managed a tiny nod. Then his eyes closed. "Tell her...I love her."

He gulped for air, then his head lolled to the side. His chest stopped rising.

"Dammit," Daniel exclaimed. "Can you do CPR?"

"He's lost too much blood. No amount of CPR will bring him back," I replied.

When I heard Katherine Bender's wailing cry, I swallowed down a knot in my throat that nearly choked me.

Daniel put his arm around my shoulder and lifted me up beside him. We stepped back together to give Katherine space. She pulled Eli's head into her lap and bent to rest her cheek against his. Her body rocked back and forth, her moans muffled by Eli's hair.

The clouds parted, allowing a wide sunbeam to spray down over Katherine as she held her son. More Amish people gathered around the pair, eyes closed and heads dropped.

The sound of the sirens seemed out of place and almost unwelcomed as the crowd grew larger. Stoic, dark-clad men stood beside women whose colorful skirts flapped out from beneath black coats. The children huddled closely to their parents, looking at the scene with frowns and sniffles.

Esta broke away from the group, running to her aunt. Not too far behind her were Verna and Mervin. The teens weren't holding hands, but anyone paying attention would see that they were a couple. Their shoulders bumped against each other until Verna gasped, covering her mouth with her hand. She sprinted forward to where Esta stood staring down at Ada Mae's remains. Esta turned into her sister's tight hug.

The girls' sorrow would lessen with time, especially after they learned the horrible things their aunt had done. For now though, it was difficult to watch.

The sirens grew louder until two ambulances drove up as far as they could into the burnt yard. People parted, allowing the medical personnel to reach the bishop and me.

Daniel's arm encircled me tighter, turning me around. I didn't protest, leaning into his warm strength. Beth and Raymond arrived first and I let them help me onto the gurney. The make-shift tourniquet Bobby had made with his coat was damp with fresh blood and I was feeling light headed. Besides my injured leg, my left shoulder thrummed painfully, probably out of joint.

Daniel held my hand as I was lifted into the ambulance, only letting go when Beth insisted he drive separately to the hospital. I managed to smile when Daniel lost the argument and stepped from the ambulance with a long face.

"I'll see you in twenty minutes," Daniel promised through the crack of the closing door.

Beth checked my pulse. "Rough day at the office?" she joked.

"Worse than most," I replied.

I relaxed back on the cushion and stared out the small window as Beth wrapped my leg in gauze.

Black smoke dotted the blue sky. The storm was moving swiftly away to the east. If I were a superstitious woman, I'd think that it had arrived to wash away Ada Mae's evil, and now that the task was complete, it was leaving.

But I wasn't superstitious. Closing my eyes, I attempted to erase the last image of Ada Mae's face from my memory. It was useless to try, though. Her pained look of regret when Eli fired the gun would haunt my dreams for a long time to come.

It was just part of the job.

28

SERENITY

"Is she still sleeping?" Todd's loud voice boomed in the room. I resisted the urge to keep my eyes closed for a little longer and opened them.

Daniel was still in the chair by the bed and Bobby sat in the one in the corner. The hospital room was brightly lit, but beyond the lone window, it was inky black.

I rubbed my eyes. "How long have I been asleep?" I asked groggily, pressing the button to raise the bed into a sitting position.

Daniel glanced at his watch. "You fell asleep right after your sister and niece left. I guess it's been about five hours."

"Why did you let me sleep so long?" I growled, my mind sparking awake.

"You were in a house that blew up. You needed your rest," Daniel retorted.

"That's right. We have everything under control. Focus your energies on healing," Bobby said.

My gaze shifted between Bobby's expectant expression and Daniel's frown. Then I looked at Todd. His usual smirk was absent for a change.

Even though I was pumped up on painkillers, my mind was clear enough to recognize Todd's desire to share news.

"What do you have for me?"

Todd walked further into the room, ignoring Daniel's narrowed eyes and his snort.

"Jenny Reynolds, the Amish driver, stopped by the office this evening. Seems after she heard about Eli dying in the explosion, she had a moment of moral clarity." He smirked and for a change, I was happy to see the obnoxious look. "She fessed up that Eli shot out the Peachey's window. She'd driven the car, thinking that by doing so, she was helping Eli protect Hannah." He rubbed his chin. "Eli shared his suspicions about Jonas with Jenny and she believed him."

I sighed. It was never as satisfying finding out the truth as I expected it to be.

"That's one more piece of the puzzle." I looked around the room. "What about Jonas? How did he take it?"

"Not very well, I'm afraid," came a feminine voice at the doorway.

I lifted my chin and craned my neck to see around Todd. Elayne smiled and walked over. Her high heels clicked on the tile floor and a flood of perfume came in with her.

I wrinkled my nose and caught Daniel grinning as he leaned back in the chair. When our eyes met, he lost the amused smile.

"How are *you* feeling?" Elayne asked, leaning on the metal frame.

I shrugged. "I've been better."

Elayne looked my face over. "It's remarkable that you weren't injured more seriously or—"

"Or killed, like Ada Mae and Eli," I finished.

"Yes, that too." She smiled at my bluntness. "Bishop Esch is in worse shape than you. He has a collapsed lung, broken collar bone and arm, and a gash across his cheek that will probably scar."

"Did you talk to him?" My curiosity rose.

She nodded. "I visited him just a moment ago. He's in decent spirits. He knows how lucky he was," she said.

"More like how blessed." I glanced at Daniel. "He told me he forgave Ada Mae for everything she'd done. He seemed to think the devil got a hold of her senses or something."

"The Amish believe in the way of grace. I'm not surprised," Daniel commented.

Elayne nodded in agreement and my chest constricted. He understood and so did Elayne. I didn't get it and probably never would.

I let the thought go, my gaze shifting back to Elayne. "From Ada Mae's own admission, she was the one who poisoned not only Robyn, Fannie and Marissa, but her mother accidentally. Jonas' unacceptable sexual conduct with a simple woman happened in another jurisdiction. We have zero reason to hold him."

Elayne puckered her lips in thought. "I was the one who told him about the explosion and his sister's death. After he asked about his daughters, he seemed relieved, almost as if Ada Mae's death freed him." She took a hesitant breath. "Don't get me wrong, he shed tears. They had a complicated relationship."

"Sick is what you mean," I said.

She shrugged. "Before I left him, he said he was planning to move back to the Black Willow settlement, once you release him."

I huffed and shook my head. Wilma was right. Jonas was an arrogant man. He expected there to be no charges against him, and now that his sister was out of the picture, he was free to pursue another relationship. Perhaps even with Marissa. My throat was suddenly dry and I swallowed the bitter taste in my mouth.

"At least he won't be our concern anymore. Regardless of his forgiving nature, I'm sure the bishop will be thrilled at the news the medicine man will be leaving us." I looked at Todd. "Go ahead and take him home. His daughters need him."

Todd nodded. "I'll see you first thing in the morning, boss."

Bobby rose from his chair. "It's going to be a long day tomorrow. I'll be heading home too."

"Thanks, Bobby." I felt the threat of tears, but kept them from falling. "For everything."

He smiled with a nod. "I think I'll keep to the mortuary and my office from now on. Being in the field today was a little more adventure than I'm used to. I'll leave it to you kids next time." He was turning to go when he stopped and looked back. "We'll have to compare notes on magical healings soon. My first one was quite extraordinary." He tipped his hat to Elayne and Daniel, and was through the door.

I raised a questioning brow at Daniel. "Hannah?" I asked.

Daniel shifted in his seat, looking uncomfortable. "Ma healed her. You don't have to believe. I saw it with my own eyes."

I recognized the hurt in his eyes. He *wanted* me to believe.

"After everything I've seen lately, I'm willing to admit there are some things that can't be explained by science. They must be miracles."

A smile spread on Daniel's lips and I smiled back.

At that moment it was just me and Daniel in the room. I'd forgotten all about Elayne standing a few feet away until she cleared her throat and I reluctantly tore my eyes from Daniel.

Elayne forced a smile. "I'll catch up with you in a few days to go over all the particulars of the case. You need to heal before we get to work."

"Are you starting the job early?" I asked, trying to keep the disappointment from my voice.

"Are you kidding me? I thought Blood Rock would be dull compared to working in the city. I was wrong. I've decided to take up Ed's offer to start next week." She tilted her head to Daniel. "I'll sign the rental papers when I return in a few days with all my things."

Daniel nodded, but didn't say anything.

The knock at the door was Elayne's cue to leave. She flashed a smile and paused in the hallway only long enough to say a few words to Hannah in Pennsylvania German and squeeze the girl's shoulder.

The nurse pushing Hannah's wheelchair raised her chin in my direction. "Are you up for another visitor?"

I didn't hesitate when I saw Hannah's puffy face. She'd been crying.

"Of course, bring her in," I directed the nurse.

When the nurse locked the wheelchair into place beside my bed, she said, "I'll wait in the hallway."

Daniel stood. "I'll be back in a minute," he said, leaving the room for Hannah's benefit.

When Hannah and I were alone, the tears began to dribble down her cheeks. I reached over, offering her my hand. She took it and squeezed.

"Did you talk to him before he died?" she said through the handkerchief she wiped her nose with.

"I did." I swallowed. "The last thing he said was that he loved you."

Hannah sucked in a breath, then calmed. She looked at me through wet eyes. "I loved him, too." She fidgeted with her fingers. "The baby's gone. I'm being punished for my sins."

I flushed with anger and sat up straighter. "No, you're not. You're only eighteen and allowed to make some bad choices." I hardened my voice. "You can't blame yourself for what Ada Mae did. She was crazy and dangerous. Unfortunately, you and Eli got caught up in her madness."

"If I had been more patient and waited for Eli to ask me to court, I wouldn't have hung out with Arlo and gotten into trouble. I wouldn't have drank the tea, and Eli wouldn't have been in the house when it exploded." A fresh round of tears slipped down her face.

"You're right, if those things hadn't happened, Eli would probably still be here. But he made his own terrible choices when he shot out the Peachey's window and then when he fired at Ada Mae in the basement. Eli wasn't an innocent bystander to a train wreck. He helped drive the train off the rails." Seeing her wide eyes, I lowered my voice. "I'm sorry, Hannah. You've had a rough time of it, no argument there, but you need to move on and begin making good choices in your life. Your mom needs you, and you have the support of the community." I hesitated. "You can stay there, can't you?"

"I'll be forgiven. It's my choice, but there will be a time of shunning for my sins," Hannah said with the hint of resentment in her words.

"Will you remain Amish?" I dared to ask.

Hannah shrugged. "I don't know. Only time will tell."

"If you ever need help, call me."

Hannah nodded.

"And stay away from Arlo Thomas. He's trouble," I advised.

Hannah's eyes glittered and I saw her stubborn nature shining though. She was one of those people who were their own worst enemy. I absorbed the tingle of apprehension on my skin.

"I'm ready to go back to my room," Hannah called out to the nurse. She looked back at me. "Momma is waiting for me."

Daniel passed Hannah as she was wheeled out.

"How did that go?" he asked.

"I'm willing to bet there's more drama on the horizon for that girl."

Daniel tilted his head and shrugged off my statement. His eyes were intense when he leaned over and kissed me lightly on the lips.

He drew back. "Are you okay?"

I took a deep breath. "My period started when I got to the hospital. I'm not pregnant."

I watched his face carefully. His eyes widened and his lips pressed together, then he nodded.

"It must be quite a relief for you," he said.

The beating of my heart slowed and my chest loosened. "Actually, it might sound weird, but I was almost sad when I came out of the bathroom earlier." His brows rose and I hurried on. "Don't get me wrong. A pregnancy would have been a disaster at this point in our relationship and my career." I took a sharp breath. "But for the first time in my life, I could see myself with a kid. You know, a family of my own."

The room was quiet except for the beeping of the monitor attached to my arm. I held my breath, wondering if I'd said way too much.

Daniel bent down and whispered, "So there's hope for us yet?"

"It's not going to be easy."

"Nothing ever worthwhile is," he said, echoing Katherine's sentiments.

His mouth closed over mine and his tongue slipped between my lips. I lifted my chin, kissing him back. Even with all my bruises and the injury to my leg, I couldn't deny the tingling sensation that spread out in my groin like warm honey. I could be near death and Daniel would still be able to turn me on.

The combination cough-throat clearing separated Daniel and me as if we were a couple of kids caught kissing behind the woodshed.

Two men walked in. The one wearing jeans and cowboy boots smiled cordially. The other wore a button up shirt and didn't bother with the show of friendliness. I could smell lawmen a mile away and I knew that beneath their blazer jackets, they each had a gun holstered.

The serious faced man had gray, thinning hair and the air of authority. The cowboy was my age and judging by his relaxed stroll into the room was the sharp shooter of the team.

"Sheriff Serenity Adams?" the older man asked out of politeness. When I nodded, he said, "I'm John Ruthers." He motioned to his partner. "This is Toby Bryant." He pushed his jacket aside just enough to reveal a shiny star on his belt loop. "We're U.S. Marshals."

I'd guessed feds, but I wasn't expecting marshals.

"Sorry I'm not in better condition to welcome you to Blood Rock. We've had a busy week, if you haven't already noticed." I couldn't keep from sounding wry. "That's my friend Daniel Bachman," I said, finishing the introductions.

The cowboy smirked, dipping his head as if to say, *yeah right, friends indeed.* The leader simply nodded dismissively. "You do have an active county for its relatively small populace and country setting," he commented.

"What can I do for you boys?" I asked, feeling the tension wafting off the men. "I thought you were in the fugitive business."

"We are. That's why we're here," John said with a small smile. "We've received information that a person we've been searching for a long time is hiding in your jurisdiction."

"Okay. Do you have a name?"

The glance that flashed between John and Toby made me question my initial judgment of who was in charge.

"His name is Jerimiah Suggs. We're pretty sure he hasn't gone by that name for years," John said.

I frowned. Their cloak and dagger bullshit was pissing me off. "Where do you want to begin looking?"

It was the cowboy who answered. "The Amish community."

CPSIA information can be obtained
at www.ICGtesting.com
Printed in the USA
LVOW04s2041061216
516057LV00011BA/1541/P